Anya backed away. "I think it's time I was in bed—"

"You're right, of course," Scott agreed smoothly, putting out a hand to cover hers as she grasped the first door handle. "Wrong room," he purred in her ear, drawing her back against his naked chest.

"I—it's very late," she tried.

"Yes, it is…far too late for either of us to back out." He nuzzled the side of her neck. "I've been thinking about this all night…and so have you."

Her head fell back against his shoulder. "I don't think I'm cut out for this kind of affair—"

"How do you know what kind of affair it's going to be until you give it a chance?" he asked. "Give *me* a chance to make love to you and you might find out that our *affair* is exactly what you need."

SUSAN NAPIER was born on St. Valentine's Day, so it's not surprising she has developed an enduring love of romantic stories. She started her writing career as a journalist in Auckland, New Zealand, trying her hand at romance fiction only after she had married her handsome boss! Numerous books later she still lives with her most enduring hero, two future heroes—her sons!— two cats and a computer. When she's not writing she likes to read and cook, often simultaneously!

Books by Susan Napier

Don't miss any of our special offers. Write to us at the following address for information on our newest releases.

Harlequin Reader Service
U.S.: 3010 Walden Ave., P.O. Box 1325, Buffalo, NY 14269
Canadian: P.O. Box 609, Fort Erie, Ont. L2A 5X3

Susan Napier

A PASSIONATE PROPOSITION

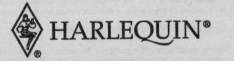

TORONTO • NEW YORK • LONDON
AMSTERDAM • PARIS • SYDNEY • HAMBURG
STOCKHOLM • ATHENS • TOKYO • MILAN • MADRID
PRAGUE • WARSAW • BUDAPEST • AUCKLAND

ISBN 0-373-12193-8

A PASSIONATE PROPOSITION

First North American Publication 2001.

CHAPTER ONE

To THE nervous girl hovering in the darkened doorway, the woman sitting at the long, scuffed dining table looked discouragingly absorbed, her slender body propped over a lecture pad as her pen danced across the ruled page. An untidy array of loose-leaf pages and open books fanned across the table-top in front of her and a half-drunk cup of tea sat forgotten at her elbow. The standard lamp which she had dragged over from the corner of the room to supplement the feeble naked bulb dangling from the ceiling poured yellow light down onto her bent head, refining the neat knot of fine, straight hair at the nape of her neck from its usual dishwater-blonde to burnished gold. Even in a boxy white shirt and fawn cargo pants she still managed to look enviously feminine.

Miss Adams had always seemed kind and approachable; she'd never shouted, or played favourites or picked on kids for things about themselves that they couldn't help, as some of the other teachers at Eastbrook did. Right now, however, her delicately etched features looked aloof in their intentness and the girl's misgivings overwhelmed her dwindling store of courage.

After all, Miss Adams was no longer teaching at Eastbrook Academy for Girls. She had left at the end of the previous year and moved out to the sticks to teach history at Hunua College, the local state high school. The fact that she was helping out on this special fifth-formers' camp during the holiday break between the first and second terms didn't mean she was ever coming back to Eastbrook. She was only here because Old Bag Carmichael had got sick and none of the

5

other teachers from school were available to come and take her place. Miss Marshall would have had to cancel the rest of the camp if she hadn't remembered that her friend and former colleague lived in the nearby town of Riverview. Luckily Miss Adams had been free to donate a few days of her time, but she certainly wasn't going to be around to help cope with any fallout from tonight's escapade—and there was bound to be *heaps* of aggro back at school if the other girls found out who had tattled, no matter that it had been out of worry rather than malice.

Clutching her loose pyjamas against her hollow stomach, the girl began to edge backwards into the gloom of the hallway, but it was too late.

As Anya turned her head to look up another reference she caught sight of a pale flutter out of the corner of her eye and was wrenched from her absorption, her heart pumping in alarm at the prospect of an intruder.

She didn't usually jump at shadows, but Anya was conscious that the regional park's accommodation was sited in a relatively isolated part of the shoreline reserve, and that she was currently the sole protector of four teenage girls. Cathy Marshall, the camp's supervising teacher, had taken the rest of the girls out with the park ranger to count and record the number of nocturnal bird-calls in the surrounding bush, part of an ongoing park survey on behalf of the Conservation Department.

Her pulse slowed in relief as she recognised the tall, gawky figure of one of her temporary charges.

'Hello, Jessica, what are you doing up?'

Glancing at her slim gold watch, Anya saw that it was well past midnight. She had been taking advantage of the quiet to catch up on some of the research which she had planned to do during these holidays and the time had passed more swiftly than she had realised.

'I…uh…' Jessica swallowed audibly, shifting her weight from one pyjama-clad leg to the other.

'Can't you sleep?' Anya asked, pitching her cool, clear voice low in deference to the night. 'Is your stomach hurting again?'

Jessica and her bunkmate had suffered a mild case of the collywobbles after gorging themselves on guava berries which they had picked off a bush hanging over a roadside fence.

Jessica blinked rapidly. 'No…uh…I just came down to…to…' She trailed off, gnawing her lower lip as her dark eyes skated around the room, searching for inspiration, '…to get a drink of water,' she finished lamely.

Anya decided to overlook the rather obvious invention.

'I see. Well, what are you waiting for?' She tilted her head towards the open kitchen door behind her. 'Help yourself.'

Returning her attention to her books, she listened as the kitchen light clicked on, and after an extended pause there came the squeak of a cupboard door, a clink of china and a gush of water. There was another long silence before the light snapped off and Jessica trailed slowly back, to linger once more in the doorway.

Anya raised her eyebrows above abstracted grey eyes, set wide apart in her delicate face. 'Was there something else?' she murmured, her mind still half on the open page in front of her.

Her impatience caused an agonised pinkening of Jessica's freckled complexion as she hurriedly shook her curly head, but her fingers continued to anxiously twist and tug at the hem of her pyjama jacket.

Anya suppressed an inward sigh and put her pen down.

'Are you sure?' she coaxed, her mouth curving in a sympathetic smile that banished the former impression of cool reserve. 'If you can't sleep, maybe you'd like to stay down here and chat for a while?' she probed gently.

An expression of yearning flitted across Jessica's uncertain face. 'Well…'

'Is there a problem with some of the other girls?'

'*No!*' Her guess had Jessica almost tripping over her tongue with an over-hasty denial. 'I mean, n-no, thanks—it's OK…really! I—I feel quite sleepy now…' She punctuated her stammered words with an unconvincing yawn. 'Uh—goodnight, Miss Adams…' She turned tail and scampered up the stairs.

Anya took up her pen again and tried to return to her research, but the memory of Jessica's anxious expression nagged at her conscience. She regretted the initial dismissiveness which had cost her the girl's confidence. Anya's ability to gain and hold the trust of her students was mentioned in her reference as one of her major strengths as a teacher. It was largely thanks to that glowing reference from Eastbrook's headmistress that she had gained her challenging new post and, after allowing herself to be persuaded to sacrifice a few days of her precious holiday to help run this camp, the least she owed her former school was to fulfil her responsibilities with good grace.

Anya had been a boarding pupil herself at Eastbrook, and was aware of the bitter feuds, petty cruelties and reckless dares that were carried out behind the house mistresses' backs. Remembering some of those escapades, she felt her guilt deepen to active unease and she pushed back her chair, gathering her books and papers up into a neat pile which she stowed in her zipped backpack. It was past time she packed up anyway. Tomorrow was the final day of the camp and the schedule was crammed full of activities, right up until the time that the bus was due to ferry the girls back to school. Then Anya would be at liberty to return to the peace and quiet of her cosy cottage. After years of sharing various accommodations she was revelling in the freedom of total independence, and these past few days of communal living had reconfirmed her belief that she had done the right thing in finally striking out on her own.

Friends and family had thought her crazy for moving to rural South Auckland and taking on a hefty mortgage at the same time as a new job, but at twenty-six Anya had felt it was time for her to take control of her life. It had been a childhood dream to live here in the countryside, and as an adult she now had the power to turn her dream into a permanent reality.

She carried her bag up to the cramped cubicle in which she and Cathy were quartered before walking quietly down the gloomy corridor towards the twin rooms the girls were sharing. She paused outside the first door, eyeing the square of pasteboard slotted into the metal holder which announced the room assignment.

Cheryl and Emma.

Her intuition hummed.

Cheryl Marko and Emma Johnson were a tiresome duo of spoiled little madams who had made it starkly plain that they were only here because the conservation camp was a compulsory part of the syllabus for boarding pupils. They had been due to go out on tonight's bird survey with the others, but Cathy had allowed them to stay behind when, coincidentally, both had complained at the last minute of severe period cramps.

Rather *too* coincidentally, Anya had thought, doling out mild analgesics to the pair as they had languished smugly in their sleeping bags while the rest of the girls clattered out on their mission.

She eased the door ajar and ducked her head inside the darkened room. A full moon pierced the gaps in the uneven curtains, casting pale bars of light over the narrow bunk beds, striping two motionless lumps in the bunched sleeping bags.

Reassured, Anya was about to withdraw when she hesitated, her grey eyes narrowing. For a couple of fashion-obsessed teenagers who constantly preened over their rake-thin bodies, they were displaying suspiciously voluptuous outlines!

Darting inside, she stripped back the hood of the first sleeping bag and stared in dismay at the untidy sausage of towels and designer-label clothes which had been used to pad out the empty interior. A quick check of the second bag yielded the same result.

Her stomach clenched in apprehension. Of course, it was quite possible that Cheryl and Emma were off on some innocent teenage escapade, but she had the sinking feeling that their sophisticated tastes wouldn't be satisfied by a common-or-garden midnight feast or giggling dorm raid.

A quick search of the rest of the empty rooms revealed no sign of the missing pair and, clinging to the slim hope that her instincts were wrong, Anya opened one final door and flicked on the overhead light.

'Girls?'

Jessica jerked bolt upright in her sleeping bag, her spectacles still perched on her nose, while in the next bed a chubby redhead rolled over onto her back, blinking blearily into the glare as she struggled into wakefulness.

'Cheryl and Emma seem to have disappeared,' said Anya crisply. 'Do either of you know where they've gone?'

She fixed her eyes on the redhead's sleep-creased face.

'Kristin? You're friends with both of them—did they say anything to you about what they were planning to do?'

'I was feeling so rotten earlier, Miss Adams, that I didn't really pay attention to what anyone was saying,' she replied plaintively.

Anya wasn't fooled by the self-pitying evasion, nor was she in any mood for a drawn-out question and answer session.

'What a pity,' she sighed. 'I was hoping to handle this on my own, but I guess I don't really have a choice. You girls should get dressed—the police will probably want a word with you—'

'The *police*?' Jessica gasped.

'B-but—shouldn't you wait a bit longer before you do anything?' gulped Kristin. 'That's what Miss Marshall would do if she was here. I mean—they'll probably turn up soon, anyway...'

'I can't take the risk—not with a beach and river nearby,' Anya said firmly. 'If I was still on staff it would be different, but I'm just an unofficial helper on this trip. I can't simply do nothing—that decision isn't mine to take. Fortunately we have their parents' phone numbers—'

It was the master stroke.

'Their *parents*?' Kristin's flush of horror almost matched her vivid hair. 'You can't call Cheryl's Dad—he'd go ballistic! They only went to a party!'

'A *party*?' Anya's heart sank even further. 'What party? Where?'

The facts that reluctantly emerged were hardly reassuring. A group of local boys who had been tossing a rugby ball around on the sand that afternoon while the girls were playing a game of beach-volleyball had extended the invitation to a party at one of their homes. Cheryl and Emma, the only ones daring enough to accept, had arranged to be picked up outside the gates of the regional park at ten o'clock by one of the boys in his car. They had been promised a ride back any time they wanted to leave the party.

Anya hid her horror. 'You mean they agreed to go off in a car with total strangers?' She racked her brains to remember exactly who she had seen on the beach. She had noticed several familiar faces from her new school, and had been able to reassure Cathy that the boys weren't a roaming gang of thugs.

'No, of course not!' Even Kristin knew the difference between reckless defiance and outright stupidity. 'It's OK, Miss

Adams—because Emma knew a couple of them from one of the bands who played at our school ball!'

Anya rolled her eyes. Oh, great…raging hormones *and* delusions of rock star grandeur!

The last straw was finding out that one of the big attractions of the party was the lack of any supervising adults.

'Emma said that this really cute guy—the one whose party it is—told her that it would be a real rave because he had the house to himself for the whole weekend,' added Jessica.

When pressed, Kristin was vague on the exact location of the party. 'The boys said it would only take about ten minutes to drive there. Some big, two-storeyed place on the other side of Riverview…'

'A white house on a hill, with a bridge at the gate and a stand of Norfolk pine trees,' added Jessica, whose memory was as sharp as her intellect.

Anya's mouth went suddenly dry and prickles of alarm feathered the back of her skull.

'The Pines?' she asked, her voice sounding shrill to her own ears. 'Was the house called The Pines?'

Kristin had turned sulky again. 'Yeah, that's it…'

'And you're *sure* about there being no adults there?'

Kristin nodded and was even more disgruntled ten minutes later as she clambered into the back seat of Anya's small car.

'I don't see why *we* have to go,' she grumbled. '*We're* not the ones in trouble.'

'Because no one's answering the phone at The Pines and I'm not leaving you two here alone while I go and get Cheryl and Emma,' said Anya as she fumbled in the glove-compartment for the wire-rimmed spectacles she used when driving and reversed the car out of the parking area. She'd left an explanatory note for Cathy, although she expected to be back well before the group returned from their survey.

Her hands tightened on the wheel as she turned from the bumpy track onto the narrow sealed road which was the main route from the coast to the suburbs of South Auckland and tried to soothe her taut nerves. She was probably overreacting. It wasn't as if she herself hadn't sneaked out to an illicit party or two during her school days—it was more or less *de rigueur* for senior boarders, and even an otherwise goody-two-shoes like Anya had been obliged to break a few rules in order to assure a peaceful life in the dorm.

The trouble was that in the four months since she had left Eastbrook she had got used to not concerning herself with after-hours student high jinks. One of the things she enjoyed about teaching at Hunua College was the separation between work and leisure. When she left school each afternoon she shrugged off her responsibilities at the gate. Oh, she took home lesson plans and piles of work to mark, but she wasn't personally responsible for the welfare of the kids themselves until the start of the next school day.

'What if they've already gone when we get there?' Jessica asked suddenly. 'What if they come back another way and we miss them?'

'This is the only road from Riverview to the regional park,' Anya told her, 'and there's very little traffic along it at this time of night, so we should notice if they pass us. Besides, Cheryl and Emma told Kristin they would be back around two, so they shouldn't have left yet—'

'Unless the party's a bust and they've gone on somewhere else,' came the sly comment from the back seat.

Anya gritted her teeth. As if she didn't have enough worries to contend with! 'Let's cross that bridge when we come to it, shall we?'

She continued to drive in tense silence. Fortunately it was a beautifully clear night, with only the suicidal dance of nocturnal insects in the high beam of her headlights to distract her from the road. The fields on either side of the unwinding ribbon of tarseal were bathed in monochromatic moonbeams and every now and then a glow of warm yellow light pinpointed a farmhouse tucked amongst a wind belt of trees, or perched on the grassy slopes of the foothills which folded themselves up against the towering shelter of the Hunua Ranges.

Ten minutes had been a macho exaggeration on the boys' part, for it was a full fifteen minutes at strictly legal speed before Anya reached the cluster of shops, houses and agribusinesses that made up the small township of Riverview.

She eased up on her speed, not even glancing in the direction of her darkened cottage, set back from the road in the large, overgrown garden which had become her personal challenge and private pleasure. Before she had gone away to school she had spent most of her childhood in a succession of inner-city hotels and apartments where the closest thing to a garden had been a potted palm.

They passed the community's one and only petrol station at the far end of the shops, its neon sign switched off and forecourt pumps locked. As buildings gave way to wire fences and trimmed hedgerows again Anya planted her foot back down on the accelerator, eager to get the coming ordeal over. She hoped that Cheryl and Emma would have the good sense to be co-operative when she fetched them away. She wanted the rescue operation to go as smoothly as possible, preferably without any dramatic scenes that might stir up more trouble than she could handle.

She didn't fancy having to deal with two recalcitrant, and quite possibly drunken, teenagers on her own, let alone a whole partyful. Although she was fit, and considered herself reasonably strong for her build, at little over five feet three inches in height she was often dwarfed by her senior students and relied on intelligence, compassion and humour to command their respect, rather than a dominating physical presence.

Her tension tightened another notch as they came over a curving rise in the road and a row of trees loomed up suddenly on the left, towering triangles of stiffly outflung branches etched darkly against the night sky in the classic Christmas tree shape. Even expecting the familiar sight, Anya felt an unwelcome leap of her pulse.

'Is this it?' Jessica's excited query was redundant as Anya braked sharply and turned off the road, the little car vibrating as its tyres rumbled over the wooden planks which bridged the deep, open drainage ditch running along the grassy verge.

At the end of a long, steeply rising sealed driveway lined with overlacing trees, they could see the big, white weatherboard house, multi-coloured lights glowing dimly behind the drawn curtains of the downstairs windows. Even with the car windows closed they could hear the heavy, rhythmic throb of a bass-beat reverberating through the walls of the house.

'No wonder they didn't hear the phone ring,' murmured Anya, pulling up behind the haphazard scatter of cars parked on the paved turning circle in front of the house.

After a brief hesitation she removed the keys from the ignition and stepped out of the car, bending down to speak through the open door. 'You two stay where you are. Lock the doors and don't open them for anyone else but me...or Cheryl and Emma. I'll be back as soon as I can. Don't get impatient if you have to wait a while, and don't get out of the car!'

Having made her point as forcefully as she could, Anya slammed the door and locked it, dropping the key into the hip pocket of her cargo pants and slipping her folded glasses into the breast pocket of her shirt as she hurried towards the sheltering portico that framed the front door.

Pushing on the doorbell brought no response. Frustrated, she tried knocking, then twisted at the ornate brass doorknob and found that it opened easily. A tentative push allowed her to step inside, where the muffled pounding which had filtered through the exterior walls escalated into an ear-crashing assault that made Anya wince.

There was little doubt she had come to the right place. There was one hell of a party going on!

Lithe young bodies were everywhere—gyrating to the music, propped against walls, sprawled over the furniture and floors; some were entwined in eye-popping embraces, others conducted point-blank conversations at shriek-level in competition with the musical cacophony. Bottles, cans, glasses and the remains of snack packets and pizza crusts seemed to litter every available flat surface. The atmosphere was hazy with cigarette smoke and thick with an aromatic combination of perfume, warm beer and sweat.

Anya threaded her way from room to room, searching for Cheryl's golden-blonde mane and the iridescent black tank-top that Kristin had said Emma was wearing, her task made more difficult by the red- and purple-coloured light-bulbs which had been screwed into the lamps, casting a murky glow over the seething figures, blending the youthful faces into an amorphous mass.

At last she spotted a familiar figure scrunched in the corner of a couch, being leered at by a lanky youth who looked unattractively worse for wear. She was grimly satisfied to note that Emma didn't appear to be enjoying herself very much.

The girl looked up as Anya approached, her pale face registering shock, disbelief and fleeting panic, swiftly superseded by an unmistakable flicker of relief.

'Come on,' Anya mouthed against the music, taking hold of her unresisting wrist and tugging her off the couch, ignoring the boy's slurred protest as she dragged his hapless companion off through the crowd.

'Where's Cheryl?' asked Anya, when she had steered her to the front door, where the noise level was slightly less brain-crushing.

Emma bit her lip, her frightened gaze darting nervously over Anya's shoulder. 'She went upstairs—a-about ten minutes ago... She said we weren't going to separate...but—but then she went up there with one of the boys who asked us to the party—Sean, he said his name was...'

A chill went down Anya's spine and a cold weight coalesced in her stomach. 'Jessica and Kristin are outside in my car. Go and get into it. Do it *now*!'

She paused only long enough to make sure the girl headed out of the door before she turned and raced up the staircase, which was clogged with people sitting on the narrow rises.

Once at the top she sped along the central hall rattling doors. Some of the rooms were locked, and in one that wasn't she flushed out false game: a giggling pair whom she sent smartly on their way. When she tried the next door it was flung open by a lone young girl with brutally short black hair bleached at the tips and a prominent nosering. Padded headphones hung around her slender neck, the wire trailing down to her bare feet.

'*What!*' she barked, hands planted on the skinny hips encased in scruffy denim jeans, her black-glossed lips peeled back in a ferocious snarl.

Anya's single-minded focus momentarily slipped at the startling image of bristling hostility.

'Ah...I'm looking for Sean,' she faltered, and was rewarded by a contemptuous narrowing of cobalt-blue eyes.

'A bit old for him, aren't you?' was the insulting response, followed by an uninterested jerk of the head. 'His bedroom's down at the far end—but the idiot's probably too trashed by now to do you any good!'

The door was slammed in her face just as suddenly as it had been whipped open, and Anya shook her head over the odd encounter as she raced down to the end of the hall.

Charging through the unlocked door, she pulled up short at the sight of the rumpled single bed where Cheryl knelt, her mouth betrayingly swollen, her clothing disarranged but thankfully still in place. Beside her on the edge of the bed sat a shirtless male in unsnapped jeans, listing heavily to one side as he drained the dregs of a small bottle of vodka and lemon mix.

Sean Monroe was one of the stars of Hunua College's first XV rugby team and had the build to prove it. Even though he was still only seventeen, his broad shoulders and thick muscles were more suggestive of a man than a boy, but the sulky defiance that appeared on his handsome face when he saw Anya confirmed he still had a lot of maturing to do.

They knew each other by sight only, since history wasn't one of his subjects, but Anya could have done without this kind of introduction. He would never forgive her for ruining his fun.

'Cheryl, are you all right?' For the second time that night Anya observed an unexpected spark of relief in the humiliated gaze of her quarry.

The girl nodded jerkily as she scrambled awkwardly off the bed, raking her tangled hair back from her face.

'He tried to make me share his drink but I didn't like the taste,' she said in a rather wobbly voice. She gave her companion a nervous look as he flopped back on the bed with a groan. 'I don't think Sean's feeling very well, Miss Adams.'

'I wonder why?' said Anya with crisp sarcasm, devoid of any shred of sympathy.

Her gaze shifted to a beer can which was doubling as an ashtray and she took a closer look at what she had assumed was a relatively innocent cigarette.

'I suppose he tried to make you share that with him, too,' she said, her voice tight with anger as she pointed at the smouldering joint.

'I only had a couple of puffs,' Cheryl defended herself. 'It just made me feel dizzy and sick to my stomach.'

Much as she longed to rail at the trembling girl for her

stupidity, Anya forced herself to swallow her blistering words. Her first priority was to get them all back to camp as quickly and quietly as possible.

She ordered Cheryl down to the car and watched cynically as the girl grabbed up her shoes and bag and scampered out, unable to believe her luck in getting away without an on-the-spot lecture. Just you wait, young lady, thought Anya grimly. Cathy was going to be furious when she was told. A lecture would be the least of Cheryl's worries!

She turned to the young man lying on the bed, intending to vent her repressed anger with a pithy few words on the subject of loutish behaviour. 'Do you realise what you were risking? That girl is under age—' she began heatedly.

Sean swore thickly and catapulted suddenly to his feet, almost knocking Anya over as he dived for the adjoining door. Incensed by his rudeness, Anya dashed after him, realising too late that she had followed him into the bathroom.

When he fell on his knees and vomited noisily into the toilet bowl she felt the first pangs of compassion, and filled a glass of water at the hand-basin to hand to him when he finished. However, when he finally staggered to his feet and took a few sips from the proffered glass he was promptly sick again, and Anya wasn't quite quick enough on her feet to prevent the front of her shirt and one leg of her trousers from being splashed.

Cursing under her breath, she grabbed a towel from the rack and scrubbed at the stains while Sean rinsed out his mouth and stumbled drunkenly back into the bedroom. Her mouth compressed as she used a second towel to quickly clean up the mess on the tiled floor, annoyed at herself for the compulsive act of neatness.

Anya's own gorge rose as she plucked at her soiled garments, her delicate nose wrinkling in fastidious horror. She couldn't sit in a small car with this sickening stench clinging to her clothes—both she and her passengers would likely be ill themselves!

Glancing out to see that Sean was slumped back on the bed, Anya bolted the bathroom door and swiftly stripped off her outer clothes. She flushed the stains in cold water, rubbing some pine-scented soap into the affected patches for good measure. The soaking pieces of fabric would be uncomfortably clammy against her skin but it was better than the noxious alternative!

She was about to wring out the excess water when she heard a crash and muffled moans on the other side of the door. Afraid that Sean had been sick again and was choking as a result, she snatched the nearest dry covering—a man's shirt that had been tossed on top of the laundry basket—and shrugged it on as she shot back into the bedroom.

She was disgusted to see Sean pawing at the rumpled covers of the bed, scrabbling for the smouldering joint which he had somehow knocked off the bedside table.

'Ah-ha!' he said, rolling over with his trophy held high, his glazed eyes barely focussing as Anya marched over, shirt flapping, and snatched the burning brand out of his clumsy fingers.

'Here, I'll take that,' she said sternly, intending to flush it down the toilet.

'Hey, no way, bitch!' He reared up and tried to grab it back. Anya jerked her arm away—he lunged, she twisted—and for a few seconds they were locked in a bizarre kind of dance at the edge of the bed, brought to an abrupt end by a deep voice, taut with outrage.

'Dammit, Sean, I thought we agreed no parties while I was— *What in the hell is going on here?*'

Anya spun around and the man who had appeared in the doorway stiffened incredulously, his cobalt-blue eyes widening in shock.

'You!'

The stunned monosyllable dripped with nameless accusation and Anya froze, her whole life flashing before her eyes.

She clutched at the gaping shirt and stared at Sean Monroe's supposed-to-be-away-for-the-weekend uncle.

Scott Tyler. Her personal demon. The man who had strongly opposed Anya's application to join the staff at Hunua College.

The legal adviser to the school board who thought that she wasn't competent to do the job she loved. The man who had admitted that he was just waiting for her to make a mistake that would prove him right!

CHAPTER TWO

IN A distant, still functioning corner of her brain Anya became aware that the music had stopped and there were sounds of high-pitched voices, car doors slamming and engines revving outside.

The party was definitely over and the reason was standing in front of them, storming mad.

She had heard via staffroom gossip that Scott Tyler had been unexpectedly landed with his sister's children while she and her husband were overseas and guessed that a thirty-two-year-old workaholic bachelor would find living with two teenagers caused a severe disruption to his formerly smoothly-running life.

Fifteen-year-old Samantha, who was in Anya's fifth-form class, was a good student but chocolate-box pretty and wildly popular with the boys, and as for Sean...well—if he had been expressly ordered not to do something then naturally he would have disobeyed, simply on principle!

Anya cleared her paralysed throat. She had no intention of being made a scapegoat for a bunch of irresponsible kids. Or shielding Sean, who had sunk back to the bed, gaping stupidly at his uncle's thunderous face.

'I can explain—' she said, gesturing vaguely in the direction of the hapless youth.

The piercing blue eyes shifted from Anya's face to the sweeping movement of her hand and she was horrified to realise that it was the one in which she held the smoking cannabis joint. She hastily whipped it behind her back.

'Don't bother. I think I get the picture—unpleasantly graphic as it is,' he said. 'How unfortunate for you that I worked double-time to complete my business early and managed to get on the last flight back from Wellington. If I'd returned tomorrow as planned you might actually have got away with it.'

The tight drawl did nothing to conceal Scott Tyler's controlled fury and Anya fought not to feel threatened by the daunting combination of his forceful personality and dominating physique.

He seemed impossibly tall from her perspective—big-boned and thick-muscled, his double-breasted grey suit accentuating his powerful build, his loosened tie hanging from the unbuttoned collar of his starched linen shirt. His sheer presence made the spacious cream-painted room feel suddenly claustrophobically small. His dark brown hair was thick and unruly, spiking over his wide forehead, his face an aggressive congregation of hard angles, with broad, high cheekbones surmounted by deep-set eyes and a handsome Roman nose that had been broken at some stage of his life. Not surprisingly, Anya thought. She had been tempted to take a punch at that arrogant nose a time or two herself...if she had been able to reach it!

He had intimidated her from their very first meeting at her personal interview with the Hunua College Board of Trustees six months ago, and in retrospect she could see that he had deliberately set out to undermine her composure. He had lounged in his seat at the end of the table, arms folded, staring at her with an unsettling intensity all through the initial part of the session, interrupting with a series of probing questions about her lack of co-educational experience just when she had begun to feel confident that she was making a good impression on the rest of the interviewing panel.

His obvious disapproval and sharply critical comments had caught her off guard and Anya had found herself floundering on the defensive. Then he had smiled—a cruelly self-satisfied curve of his hard mouth—and her innate stubbornness had kicked in. Her slender spine had stiffened as she revealed her grace under fire, retaliating with a calm, level-headed self-assurance combined with a dry sense of humour which had clawed back the lost ground. For a while, though, she had felt like a prisoner in the dock, and she hadn't been surprised to later find out that Scott Tyler was one of South Auckland's leading barristers, with a reputation for winning difficult cases on the strength of his ruthless cross-examinations.

From the brief research she had done after applying for the job, she knew that, although he wasn't a voting member of the board, his role as legal consultant and a personal friendship with the Chairman gave him a considerable amount of influence.

Fortunately, the headmaster, Mark Ransom, had firmly thrown his support behind Anya as the best of the three other candidates already interviewed, and a majority of the board must have concurred, for several days later Anya had been overjoyed to receive the job offer that had precipitated her move to Riverview.

To her dismay, accepting defeat graciously was evidently not one of Scott Tyler's famed accomplishments, and at each successive encounter, despite her strenuous efforts to be pleasant, they'd seemed to end up on opposite sides of an argument.

Which made it even more important that this silly incident not be blown out of proportion.

'I know what it looks like, Mr Tyler, but you're jumping to the wrong conclusions—' she protested as he turned his attention back to his slack-jawed nephew, grimly assessing the extent of his intoxication.

'I've had a hellish twenty-four hours with some very stroppy clients and I'm not in the mood to handle any more nonsense right now. So I suggest you put your clothes back on and get out,' he tossed harshly over his shoulder, using the same menacing tone which had cleared out the rowdy party-goers below in record time. 'I want to talk to my nephew—*alone*. I'll deal with *you* later!'

Anya would have been delighted to escape, but she wasn't going to leave with that ominous threat hanging over her head.

'Look, I understand that you're pretty annoyed about Sean throwing a party without your permission—'

He jerked around, snarling like a wounded bear. 'How perceptive of you!'

'—but I only found out about it myself about half an hour ago,' she finished stoutly, bracing herself as he prowled back to where she stood. She dug her toes into the carpet, determined not to give ground.

'So you immediately rushed over to strip and join in the fun?' he savaged with brutal sarcasm. 'I had no idea that history teachers were so *progressive…*'

His raking look of contempt made her clear, honey-gold skin bloom with unwelcome fire. Her grey eyes darkened with reproach, which only seemed to feed his smouldering fury.

'Is this one of the methods of "inspiring young minds" that you talked of bringing to the college?' Up close she could see the small scar on the left corner of his narrow upper lip, the one that gave him such an impressive sneer. 'How long have you been offering private lessons in practical sex education as a part of your curriculum?'

'Don't be ridiculous!' she cried, struggling to remain reasonable in the face of his flagrant provocation. There was no point in both of them losing their tempers. She had noticed it was a popular tactic of his—playing devil's advocate, needling people until they became too annoyed to think straight, let alone consider the wisdom of their words. Maintaining control was the key to surviving a verbal encounter with Scott Tyler.

'This is just a set of unfortunate circumstances—' she

stated clearly, tilting her head up in the unconsciously haughty gesture that she had inherited from her flamboyant mother.

'That's what they all say.' His cynical laugh was gritty with scorn. 'The "unfortunate circumstances" usually involve getting caught red-handed at the scene of the crime. I'm a criminal lawyer, remember—I've heard every excuse in the book.'

'And who better than a lawyer to know that appearances can be deceptive?' she snapped back.

'In your case I'd agree…very deceptive. Who'd have thought that the quiet and refined Miss Adams, with her modest hemlines and sensible shoes, would have a penchant for see-through underwear and seducing her students…'

'I was *not* seducing anyone!' spluttered Anya, unable to refute the underwear allegation. For the most part her clothes were classically simple and tasteful, as required of a role-model for impressionable teenagers, but since her slender figure required only the bare minimum of support she didn't have to be practical when it came to buying lingerie. She was free to indulge her secret passion for gossamer-thin lace and frivolous frippery. As long as she was well covered up she considered it no one's business but her own what she chose to wear under her clothes.

Only right now she was feeling very much undercovered and a trifle cool, despite the heat in her cheeks. Glancing down, she saw that the oversized white shirt she was trying to anchor one-handed across her scantily clad body was made of slippery, ultra-fine silk through which it was possible to see the sheer lace of her low-cut emerald bra and matching panties.

'Really…so you just like to prance around half-naked at parties for your own entertainment? You obviously find it sexually arousing to be the focus of male attention,' he taunted, his sardonic stare making her supremely conscious of the way her nipples had tingled to hardness against the twin layers of flimsy fabric. 'That's tantamount to seduction in my book.'

'Then your book would be wrong!' She might have known that he would draw attention to something any real gentleman would have politely ignored. How dared he imply that she found *him* attractive? 'There's a cool breeze coming through the window behind me, in case you haven't noticed!' she pointed out obliquely.

His blue eyes glinted with malice and she hurried on before he could make another devastating comment.

'For goodness' sake, you can't think I took my clothes off because I *wanted* to—'

His face hardened, his whole body contracting with a dangerous tension. 'Are you claiming that Sean tried to rape you?' he ground out.

'No, of *course* I'm not!' she cried, frankly appalled at the direction of his thoughts. One side of the shirt slipped from her distracted fingers and she frantically brought up her other hand to try and overwrap the fabric into more concealing folds.

His hostile preparedness had eased at her shocked exclamation but now his hand shot out and enveloped her fragile wrist in a steely grip.

'Watch what you're doing, woman! For God's sake, give that to me before you singe a hole in one of my best shirts.' He extracted the stubby remains of the mangled joint and let her go, crushing out the still-burning tip with his bare fingers.

'*Your* shirt?' She rubbed her buzzing wrist, goose-pimples breaking out over every centimetre of bare skin being caressed by the borrowed silk. 'I— it was in the bathroom—I assumed it was Sean's...' she stammered.

A vein pulsed in his temple and a possessive growl sounded at the back of his throat. 'What—it's not enough that you play lord of the manor to your friends when I'm away, you have to dress the part, too?' He sent his nephew, who was just getting unsteadily to his feet, a wrathful look that had him plopping heavily back down on his backside. 'When I said I was happy to look after you and Sam for a few weeks, I didn't envisage it meant opening up my wardrobe to you, as well!'

He screwed up the final shreds of cannabis cigarette in his contemptuous fist and scattered the dusty debris out of the open window.

'Is there any more where that came from?' he demanded of Anya.

'I have no idea,' she said succinctly, still grappling with the knowledge that she was wearing his shirt. It made her feel strangely shivery, uncomfortably vulnerable to him in a way that it was difficult to define. 'It wasn't mine. I've never smoked marijuana in my life.'

A tug of his scar hitched his lip into a disbelieving curl. 'You're telling me you never ran across any illicit weed when you were a pupil at that exclusive upper-crust school of yours? Places like Eastbrook are a hotbed of experimentation—WASPy little rich girls doing the rebellion thing, or getting high as a way of punishing mummy and daddy for being too busy with their own lives to pay them enough attention; bored young things always on the lookout for kicks, with easy access to money and no one to really care how they spend it—'

'There's that kind of element in every school, no matter what social strata it serves,' Anya said, stung by the sneering accuracy of his thumbnail sketch. 'And I never said I hadn't come across it, only that I hadn't used it.'

'Come to think of it, cannabis is probably a little low rent for the privileged elite,' he jeered. 'Maybe the junior jet-set prefer designer drugs to go with their designer clothes.'

Now he was going too far! Anya's quiet temper bubbled

to the surface. His entire attitude was in need of serious re-adjustment!

'You have a real chip on your shoulder, don't you?' she burst out. 'Let me guess: your parents couldn't afford to send you to a private school, so you resent anyone who was given the educational and social advantages that you weren't. Well, most young kids don't have any more choice about where they go to school than you did—I certainly didn't!

'And, contrary to your obvious prejudice, Mr Tyler, private school pupils aren't all elitist snobs who take their privileges for granted and look down their noses at the rest of the world. A lot of them are the children of ordinary, egalitarian, hard-working New Zealanders who believe in the kind of discipline, or moral and religious values that aren't offered at a state school.'

She unthinkingly punctuated her lecture with a teacher's wagging finger, and Scott Tyler reacted with the insulting slyness of a naughty schoolboy.

'Careful, Miss Adams, your slip is showing,' he mocked, his gaze dipping down to where her emerald bra-strap peeked from under the sliding collar of his shirt.

She hitched it impatiently back into place with a baleful look, refusing to be diverted. 'My qualifications are rock-solid—it's because of your own reverse snobbery that you didn't want me getting the teaching position at the college. You did everything you could to cast me into a bad light at my interview, and it sticks in your craw that they gave me the job anyway!'

The glow of smug triumph on her delicate face was like a red rag to a bull.

'I didn't want you in the job because I didn't think you were physically or mentally tough enough to cope with the pressures and problems of teaching in a big unisex school which draws a large number of its students from a lower socio-economic group,' he grated, planting his hands on his hips, his open jacket revealing the flatness of his tailored waistcoat against his hard stomach. 'And I still don't!'

Anya bristled. 'There are plenty of other female teachers on the staff—' she said pugnaciously.

'—who've got previous experience in a variety of large unisex schools, whereas you've been insulated in your cushy little Academy for Young Ladies ever since you graduated from training college.'

She lifted her silky-fine eyebrows, echoing his taunting mockery from a few moments ago. 'Careful, Mr Tyler, your inferiority complex is showing.'

He bared even white teeth in the opposite of a smile. 'So the butterfly can bite? Insulting me won't change the facts.'

He saw her as a butterfly? She pictured herself as a small but determined terrier.

'The facts being that so far I've been managing my classes just fine!' Apart from a few natural hiccups she'd rather not mention.

'It won't last,' he predicted bluntly.

'Are you threatening me?'

'Do I have to? If tonight is an example of how you "manage" your students I think the major threat is your own behaviour.'

She compressed her lips, controlling the surge of indignant words that welled hotly in her throat. After his disparaging comments about her former school her explanation wasn't going to go down too well, so she delivered it in edited highlights.

'Look, this really doesn't have to go any further,' she said, adopting her most reasonable tone. 'I'm helping supervise a holiday camp out at the regional reserve, and a couple of the girls came to the party without permission, so I drove over to pick them up. I tracked them down but then Sean was sick all over my clothes. I was cleaning up in the bathroom when

I heard him knock something over and ran back in to check…'

She looked over at the culprit, meeting his bloodshot brown eyes behind his uncle's back. She had half expected him to try and bluster his way out of trouble, but perhaps he was too intoxicated to put together a coherent sentence. Or maybe he was just hoping that by keeping silent he could avoid incriminating himself

'Is that what happened, Sean?' Scott Tyler rapped out, inclining his head but not taking his sceptical gaze off Anya.

The boy shrugged, but he wasn't too strung out to miss that the cynical edge in the gravelly voice wasn't directed his way.

'How should I know why she invited herself?' he mumbled quickly, his sluggish tongue tangling in the consonants. 'It was a party, man…chicks have been coming and going all night.'

A cold trickle of dismay ran down Anya's spine when she saw him leaning back out of his uncle's peripheral sight, smirking maliciously at her.

'All I know is, she followed me into my room and wouldn't leave me alone. Who'da known she was so hot? Ever made it with a history teacher, Unc'l Scott?'

The grubby insinuation with its macho, man-to-man overtones had Anya's eyes snapping back to Scott Tyler's face, which was suddenly rigidly impassive, wiped clean of all emotion. She guessed it was the expressionless mask he wore into the courtroom, when he didn't want anyone to know what he was thinking.

'Whatever he's implying didn't happen,' she said tartly. 'You know very well he's just telling you what he thinks you want to hear…'

One thick, dark eyebrow shot up. 'Is he?'

He was just playing devil's advocate, she told herself.

'You know he is. Look out the window if you don't believe me. The girls I came here to find are down there waiting for me in my car—'

He sent a fleeting, almost uninterested, glance down towards the turning circle. 'There's no smoke without fire,' he murmured with infuriating blandness.

'What are you—a fireman now?' she flung at him witheringly, her slender body vibrating with fury. 'I thought you were supposed to be a hot-shot lawyer. Why don't you act like one and make Sean tell you the *real* truth!'

'His version, or yours? When there's two witnesses, the truth is often a matter of perspective.'

It was on the tip of Anya's tongue to tell him that she had another witness, but she didn't want to involve Cheryl, and thus Eastbrook, unless she could help it.

'Are you saying that you actually *believe* him!'

'You must admit I've ample reason to be suspicious. Don't tell me you aren't aware that there's something inherently erotic about a woman wearing a man's shirt,' he said, his eyes sliding down over her silk-wrapped body in a speculative way that made her blood boil, and not entirely with fury. 'And the little white socks add just the right provocative touch of pseudo-innocence.'

'Oh, for goodness' sake, don't be ridiculous!' A piercing thrill of guilty pleasure made Anya lash out, trying to douse the treacherous feelings aroused by his words with a drenching of pure scorn. 'I suppose you're going to accuse me of trying to seduce *you* next!'

There was a short, electric silence as they stared at each other, and Anya noticed all the things about him she had always tried very hard *not* to notice: the smooth grain of his olive skin as it stretched over the strong bones of his face; the almost feminine lushness of the thick dark lashes which framed his compelling blue eyes, and the strikingly masculine contrast of that thin, yet sensual mouth, and harshly chiselled jaw.

The stubbly regrowth of his beard and faint purplish tinge under his sunken eyes—signs of his 'hellish' day—made him look rakish rather than merely weary.

When he spoke again his voice was deeper, softer, and more dangerous than she had ever heard it. Too soft for the boy behind him to hear. And he allowed a flare of male hunger to show in the deep blue gaze.

'You're welcome to try, but I should point out that I'm a great deal more discerning—and considerably more demanding—than your average randy teenager...'

The sheer wickedness of the barbed challenge sucked the breath out of her lungs, and Anya opened and closed her mouth several times before she summoned the words to prove that she was wasn't totally vanquished.

'Oh, you're impossible! It's easy to see you're related—you're both as bad as each other. Believe what you damned well like; *I* don't care!'

And on that resounding lie Anya swung on her heel and stormed into the bathroom, slamming the door violently enough to cause the mirror to shiver on the wall above the basin and several toiletries to fall over on the vanity top.

Muttering to herself to bolster her sense of outrage, she ripped off the silk shirt and pulled on her wrinkled clothes, the damp patches practically sizzling as they hit her burning skin. She finished zipping up her ankle boots with a vicious tug that jammed a piece of her sock in the meshing teeth and swore through tight lips as she tried to work it free.

She had always thought of cotton ankle socks as utilitarian rather than sexy, but now that serene unawareness was gone for ever. She would never be able to put on a pair of white socks again without thinking of *him*.

He had viewed them as *provocative*, for God's sake! A pair of simple, inexpensive white socks! The man was plainly in need of therapy, she thought as she checked herself out in the mirror, looking in vain for the cool, capable, down-to-earth Miss Adams she was used to recognising in her reflection.

With her glittering, storm-darkened eyes, flushed cheeks, and the baby-fine wisps of hair escaping from the pins at her nape and drifting forward to curve around her smooth oval jaw, she looked disturbingly young and flustered. Not in control.

And she had no make-up to repair the damage to her self-image. She did what she could, smoothing back the strands of hair from her glowing forehead and tucking them firmly into place with tremulous fingers. Had her small mouth always looked that rosy and full? She pressed her lips together in a stern line and willed her colour to fade back to normal. She could do nothing about the way her clothes clung where they were wet, but at least they were clingy in fairly non-strategic areas.

She could hear a low murmur coming from the bedroom and she hesitated for a moment before she squared her shoulders, gathered up her ragged dignity, and reached for the door.

She was going to walk back out there with her head held high, and if fault should be admitted she was prepared to be graciously forgiving, as befitted her normally kind and compassionate nature.

But the sight that met her eyes wasn't promising. Scott Tyler stood beside his seated nephew, his hand resting on Sean's brawny bare shoulder, whether for reassurance or restraint, she wasn't sure.

'Well, has he told you what happened?' she challenged.

Scott Tyler's unreadable mask was firmly back in place

'That could take some time in his present condition,' he said uninformatively, acknowledging the condition of her clothes with barely a flicker of his eyes. His voice flattened into resolute finality. 'As I said before, it's late, and if there are issues to be settled they can wait until a more civilised hour...'

He dropped his hand and moved towards her, obscuring her vision of the boy, imposing himself squarely in the centre of her attention. He was definitely in full protective mode, she decided, and in the split second before his broad chest blocked out her view her heart sank to see that the smirk had returned to the teenager's face. The obnoxious weasel wasn't going to accept responsibility for his actions until he was sober enough to appreciate the true consequences of his lies.

'Well, here's one issue that can be settled right now,' she announced, pulling at a clammy spot on her cotton shirt where it had moulded transparently to her skin. 'As you can see for yourself, I'm going to have to get my clothes cleaned. I'll be sure and send you the bill.'

His thick lashes veiled his expression as he studied the effect of her makeshift laundering.

'By all means. But don't expect me to pay it if there's contributory negligence involved,' he told her in that same flat, non-negotiable tone. 'For all I know you could have dunked them just now in the bathroom, to give credence to your story.'

Anya forgot about being kind and compassionate.

'I suppose being exposed to the seamy underbelly of society all the time has given you a very nasty and obsessively suspicious mind, and distorted your view of the way normal, *innocent*, people behave,' she said, with a cutting disdain that was designed to make him cringe.

He didn't cringe, but he did back off slightly, leaning a broad shoulder against the painted frame of the casement window in concession to his weariness. 'I prefer to think of it as trusting to the wisdom of experience. As a history teacher you must believe in using the lessons of the past to avoid repeating future mistakes.'

Her mouth primmed in frustration, for she hated to admit

he was right, and for the first time he showed a glimmer of untainted amusement, a faint kick of his mouth which delivered a corresponding kick to Anya's pulse. His next words were also guaranteed to raise her blood pressure.

'So be careful you're not making a mistake, Miss Adams, by riling me when I've already told you I'm in a *very* bad mood. Your position at the moment is rather untenable. It could be construed as contributing to the delinquency of a minor, for example...'

She was quick to scorn his bluff. 'Apart from the fact that the whole accusation is nonsense—he isn't a minor.'

He was about to offer a caustic reply when something outside the window snagged his attention. 'Are you sure you want to argue the point now? Because the natives down there seem to be getting restless...'

She frowned at him, suspecting a trick. 'What?'

'There are two girls getting out of a yellow hatchback I presume is yours,' he said, looking out the window. 'They seem to be debating whether to approach the house—'

Anya yelped and flew over to see that he was right. Oh, God, she had been so distracted by his presence that she had completely forgotten about the girls! Supposedly her prime consideration on this mission.

She clutched the windowsill, gazing down in dismay as Jessica and Kristin milled uncertainly around the side of the car. Hadn't she *told* them not to get out?—but of course by now they must be starting to panic at her extended absence.

'Perhaps you'd like me to invite them up to join us while we finish the discussion you seem so keen on prolonging...' came a silky purr.

'*No!*' Anya was too busy castigating herself to notice his openly baiting tone. She could just imagine what four gossipy girls would make of the pernicious scene. She looked at her watch, her thoughts fixated on damage control. If she didn't get back to camp before Cathy read her note, all hell was likely to break loose. Or, should she say, *further* hell?

She glared at the cause of her appalling lapse in judgement. 'I have to go—'

'Oh, what a pity,' he said, his voice dripping with sarcasm. 'Just when I was about to offer you a cup of tea.'

She scowled. Naturally he would see her strategic retreat as his victory. 'When you get *him* sober enough to tell you that my presence here was entirely innocent—' she said, nodding in Sean's direction as she hurried towards the door '—I'll expect to receive a sincere apology. From *both* of you! And we'll consider that an end to the matter.'

She thought that she had succeeded in having the last word, but a surly remark referring to frigid temperatures and the devil's abode floated downstairs in her wake, making her itch to turn around and hit back with an equally vulgar blow. She managed to cling to her decorum but only by locking up her jaw. For a non-violent person she was beginning to have some very disturbing thoughts. All to do with *That Man*.

'Where were you, Miss Adams? We were getting worried,' said Jessica, as Anya herded the girls back into the car and burnt rubber down the drive in her anxiety to escape the invisible laser-beam eyes she was sure she could feel drilling into her back.

'We saw that big guy go in and break up the party but you didn't come out with the others. He looked pretty mad when he drove up and saw all the cars. I bet he went totally psycho at his kid for having a party,' said Kristin in suppressed excitement. 'I bet there was a big fight. Is that what took you so long, Miss Adams?'

'You don't—want—to—know,' Anya ground out through her still-clenched teeth, her usually gentle voice so awe-inspiringly crabby that there was dead silence all the rest of the way back to the camp, apart from the occasional frightened sniffle from Emma and Cheryl in the back seat as they contemplated their uneasy future.

CHAPTER THREE

ANYA had a mildly thumping head when she arrived back at the regional reserve, and by the time she drove home the next afternoon it had developed into a full-blown tension headache.

She was just grateful that the decision of what to do with the chastened pair of miscreants had not fallen on her own shoulders. The two girls had produced copious amounts of penitent tears for a livid Cathy Marshall, who had raked them severely over the coals and segregated them out to do all the most boring, arduous and least-liked of the clean-up jobs rostered for the last day.

Seeing Cheryl scraping out the burnt-on muck of ten days of inexpert cooking from the camp oven and Emma mopping floors and grimacing over the application of a toilet brush had given Anya hope that their too-ready expressions of remorse might actually turn into a genuinely felt regret for their misdeeds.

But executing summary punishment hadn't solved Cathy's basic dilemma of whether to consider the offence a trivial one satisfactorily dealt with on-the-spot, as was her first impulse, or to put the girls on report to the headmistress when they returned to school, in recognition of the potential danger they had posed to themselves and to the Academy's reputation.

Anya couldn't blame her friend for wanting to avoid any official black mark against the camp, but did point out that once their initial fright wore off the girls were unlikely to refrain from boasting about their adventure. If it became common knowledge at the school, it would inevitably reach Miss

Brinkman's ears and she would want to know why she hadn't been kept fully informed.

When she got on the bus back to Eastbrook, Cathy was still worrying about what to gloss over and what to emphasise in her written report, having reluctantly come to the conclusion that she couldn't entirely leave it out.

'I could probably get away with just using my discretionary judgement if it wasn't for the fact that you found Cheryl with the boy, and you think there might have been some marijuana around,' she sighed. 'But don't worry, nothing I say is going to reflect badly on you, Anya,' she hastened to add. 'You did the school a huge favour by helping out these last few days. It was just bad luck that those wretched girls took off when you were there by yourself. I'm going to tell Miss Brinkman you did exactly what I would have done in the same circumstances...'

Not quite. For Anya hadn't gone into the full, gory details of her humiliating encounter with Scott Tyler. She had merely said that he had arrived after she had sent the girls out to the car, and that he had been angry and rude. She hadn't wanted to add to Cathy's anxieties by telling her of the personal hostility that had flared out of control during the confrontation, especially when her friend had instantly recognised the name of her protagonist.

'Scott Tyler—the lawyer? The one who got that body-in-the-bag murderer—sorry, *alleged* murderer—off?' Cathy was impressed enough to be momentarily diverted from her troubles. 'Wow, I've seen him on the TV news—he's one tough-looking dude. According to the papers he made absolute mincemeat of a watertight case to get that verdict. You definitely wouldn't want to get on the wrong side of an argument with *him*!'

Tell me about it! Anya had thought. When they had finally got to bed she had tossed and turned sleeplessly for what had remained of the night, running and rerunning her mental vid-

eotape of the experience, thinking of how differently the sce-
nario would have played if she hadn't let herself be side-
tracked by his angry assumptions, and inventing pithy replies
to his insults that she wished she had been able to think of
at the time.

In the cold light of day she could almost convince herself
that it had been a simple case of overreaction on both sides.
Once Scott Tyler's temper had cooled and he was no longer
hampered by fatigue he was bound to take a more reasonable
view. Surely the cynical lawyer in him would soon conclude
that Sean's spiteful words had simply been a drunken attempt
to save his own skin?

He might even be content to act as if the whole unfortunate
incident had never occurred. Anya certainly would. In spite
of her defiant departing words she would prefer not to have
to raise the subject with him ever again.

It would be hard enough having to face him next time they
met. Scott Tyler had seen her *underwear*, for God's sake!
The last time that had happened was on her twenty-first birthday, and the man involved had gone on to break her heart.
Not a very happy precedent!

Her nervous brooding made the last few hours of the camp
stretch and sag like tired elastic and she was glad to finally
be able to wave the air-conditioned bus onto the road back
to Auckland and hop into her little car.

The hot bands of iron tension compressing her temples
began to ease as she pulled into her crushed gravel driveway
and parked in the small garage attached to the side of the
weatherboard cottage.

She had bought the two-bedroomed house a few weeks
after she'd signed her employment contract with Hunua
College, rationalising that even if the job didn't work out as
she expected there were plenty of other secondary schools
scattered around South Auckland that were within reasonable
commuting distance of Riverview. As it was, the college was

only half an hour's drive along the winding rural roads to the sprawling outskirts of suburban south Auckland.

The house had been an early Christmas present for herself, and although it had put her deeply in debt to the bank she relished the long-term commitment the monthly payments represented. People—her cosmopolitan parents included—had told her that buying property in a small rural town was a poor investment, but they didn't seem to appreciate that to her this wasn't an investment, it was her *home*, a place for her to put down roots and flourish, emotionally as well as physically. Even several months after she had moved in she still felt a sharp thrill of joy each time she came home, to know that she was the proud owner of her own little quarter-acre of paradise.

'Hello, George. Have you come to welcome me home?' She bent to stroke the lean ginger cat which appeared from nowhere to wind around her ankles as she unloaded her bags from the boot. The ginger tom was actually a stray who considered the whole neighbourhood his personal territory, granting his fickle attentions to whomever was likely to provide him with the choicest titbits at any given time.

Anya scratched his bent ear and smiled at his motoring purr, her face lighting up from within, the spontaneous warmth lending her quiet features a glowing enchantment.

Now that she was feeling thoroughly settled in she had been thinking she might get herself a cat of her own. Or even a dog. Thanks to her childhood asthma and her opera singer mother's horror of anything that might compromise her respiratory tract and thus her peerless voice, she had never been allowed to have a pet. The frequent international travelling associated with her mother's career had precluded even a goldfish, and only during her precious holiday visits to her aunt and uncle's dairy farm at Riverview had Anya been able to indulge her interest in animals—with nary a sneeze or wheeze in sight!

'Let's see if I can't find a nice can of tuna for us to share,' said Anya, following George up the narrow brick path that she had laid herself, bordered by the flower beds already dug over in preparation for planting out. Although it was still unseasonably warm for mid-April, the clouds were gathering over the Hunua Ranges and she could scent a hint of rain in the sultry air.

Once inside she kicked off her shoes with a sigh of relief and went around opening the windows to air out the stuffy rooms. It was too early for her evening meal but she carefully divided up a tin of tuna and set down a saucerful on the kitchen floor for George while she tossed the rest with the salad ingredients she had picked up from a roadside stall on the way home and put it in the fridge for when she got out of the bath.

She intended to have a glorious, long, hot, mindless soak in lavender-scented water to steam out all the weary kinks in her body and the nagging worries in her brain. Then she would have her solitary salad with a glass of crisp white wine and relax amongst her books, with perhaps a delicate piece of Bach on the stereo. Oh, the bliss of being free of rules and regulations, and the obligation to be considerate of the rights of others. She didn't even have to worry about how deep to fill the old-fashioned bath, for there was no one to moan if she selfishly used up all the hot water.

Leaving George licking his chops over the empty saucer and eyeing the rush mat by the back door where he invariably liked to curl up and digest her largesse, Anya ran her bath and sank into it with a groan of sybaritic pleasure.

But the bath wasn't the total escape from reality she had expected it to be, for as the enervating heat sank into her tired bones and the fragrant steam wreathed her face in dew, Anya's drifting thoughts circled relentlessly back to the annoying subject of Scott Tyler.

How was it he always managed to get her in tongue-tied knots?

When they had first been introduced she had had fond hopes of their establishing a friendly connection.

She had been welcomed to her afternoon interview in the college boardroom by the chairman of the board, a grizzled man in his sixties, and they had still been shaking hands when he'd suddenly beamed over her shoulder.

'Oh, good, there you are, Scott! I wondered if you were going to make it back in time to sit in on this last one. Come and meet our final candidate—the lass from Eastbrook. We've already talked over her credentials...' He performed a rather perfunctory introduction, distracted from his task by the throaty laugh from the tall, svelte brunette attached to Scott Tyler's arm.

'Sorry, Daddy,' said the woman, giving him an unrepentant buss on the cheek. 'I'd just finished a case in the district court so I buzzed Scott on his cell-phone and took him out to lunch. He and I got to talking shop and the time just slipped away from us.'

'Heather works for a big law firm in the city,' Hugh Morgan explained to Anya with fatherly pride, giving her the excuse to turn away from the jolting connection with a pair of unusual, electric-blue eyes. 'Does heaps of Crown prosecutions. Very clever girl. Came top of her year at law school.'

'Oh, Daddy, that was a little while ago now,' Heather Morgan fluttered with a coy modesty that didn't quite gel with her seriously elegant suit and ambitious air of self-importance. Anya estimated the 'girl' to be somewhere in her early thirties. That coy 'little while' was likely to be more than a decade ago, she thought with uncharacteristic bitchiness.

'You know I don't like to rest on my laurels,' she continued, casting a teasing sideways glance out of her dark almond eyes at the imposing man at her side. 'Especially with Scott around to keep me on my toes.'

She finally directed a condescending smile at Anya in belated acknowledgement of her reason for being there. 'So you're a schoolteacher?' Her bored inflection made it sound like the most dreary and uninspiring job on earth.

Anya inclined her head politely, keeping her tongue behind her teeth as she was wished an insipid good luck. She was amused rather than offended by the woman's arrogant assumption of superiority. The fact that she had graduated her history degree with first-class honours and won a scholarship to Cambridge which she had waived in order to train as a teacher, would doubtless cut no ice with Miss Morgan. Like Anya's parents she would probably just consider it a pathetic waste of potential; because there was no serious money to be made in teaching, no important status to claim, no high-profile perks and rewards for a job well done. Just a quiet satisfaction at having helped guide and expand the minds of future generations of lawyers and teachers.

Anya stood quietly by as the other three continued to exchange personal pleasantries, trying not to let her nerves show, only stirring when she heard a passing reference to Scott Tyler's home.

'You live at a property called The Pines?' she was startled into saying. 'Not the house that's on the road out to Riverview?'

'Yes, that's it.' Scott Tyler looked down at her, the clipped wariness of his words emphasised by a hint of cool reserve in his eyes.

'Have you driven past it? Charming, isn't it? He bought it about…five years ago, didn't you say it was, darling?' Heather Morgan was more forthcoming, deftly making it clear that their relationship was not only professional. 'Mind you, he says it was in a pretty run-down state at the time— the absentee landlord hadn't bothered with anything but basic maintenance for years—so Scott's had it completely redecorated inside and out since then.'

'If it was five years ago then you must have bought it from a close relative of mine,' Anya told Scott Tyler eagerly, delighted at the prospect of a common point of interest that might help individualise her in his eyes during the next hour of question-and-answer. 'Kate Carlyle. She was over here from London to accept an offer on the house. I'm sure you'd remember if you had met her. She's an extremely striking woman—rather famous in America and Europe as a concert pianist...'

He had stiffened slightly. Did he suspect her of being a shameless name-dropper? Well, perhaps so on this occasion—but she was also genuinely proud of Kate's brilliant achievements.

'Oh, yes, I remember Kate Carlyle,' he said, his deep, harsh voice banked with unidentifiable emotion. No doubt, then, that the meeting had been memorable. Even when she wasn't trying, Kate always had a big impact on men. 'Exactly how closely are you related?'

'She's my cousin on my mother's side,' she said happily, tilting her small face to meet his demanding gaze.

His expression tightened in what she took to be suppressed scepticism. 'And how much—or how little—do you have in common with your famous *cousin*?'

Her rueful smile forgave him for having doubts. He was obviously too polite to wonder out loud how such a beautiful, glamorous and talented creature as Kate could be related to plain, unremarkable Anya Adams, who didn't have an artistic bone in her body—much to her parents' enduring disappointment!

'Well, since we're both living on opposite sides of the world we very rarely see each other any more,' she admitted, 'and Kate does a lot of travelling, but we're still family so we naturally try to keep in touch.' At least Anya did. She supposed the occasional rushed few lines of e-mail from Kate in belated response to a long, newsy, handwritten letter from herself could be considered an effort, however feeble, to keep in touch.

'That doesn't really answer my question, does it?' he drawled, with a sardonic twist of his mouth. 'Perhaps I should have phrased it differently…asked if you share similar character traits, and perhaps her personal philosophy of life…?'

Anya was bewildered. She wasn't sure quite where his question was supposed to be leading, and it was obvious from his mocking expression that he was ready to pounce on any response.

What on earth did he want her to say? As far as she was aware Kate wasn't of any particular philosophical bent—unless you counted her dictum of 'music first'. Whatever else Kate might be, she was a consummate professional.

'Well, considering our shared background I guess a certain similarity is inevitable,' she ventured cautiously. 'When Kate was orphaned she came to live with my parents and me. For a while we were brought up together, just like sisters.' With Kate being the senior by four years, and very much the dominant one, already obsessed by music and not at all patient with the childish preoccupations of her eight-year-old cousin.

'So, you're sisters under the skin?' he confirmed with a hint of contempt, paraphrasing her words in a way that gave them a whole different meaning.

For some reason, the closer the kinship she claimed with Kate, the less Scott Tyler seemed to be impressed. Did he think she was exaggerating her own importance in order to curry favour? Did he perceive it as an indication of a sense of personal inadequacy on her part—one that might affect her authority of her students?

Disconcerted by his rising antipathy, Anya let her nerves run away with her tongue.

'I suppose you were told when you bought it that the original part of your house is over eighty years old...and that it was built by John Carlyle—Uncle Fred's father.' History being her professional forte and personal interest, it was a natural subject for Anya to fall back on in moments of uncertainty. 'Did Kate mention that she inherited The Pines after her parents were killed when she was only twelve? Of course, it was a working farm back then and it was leased as a share-milking operation by the estate until Kate was old enough to decide what she wanted to do with it. She sold off most of the grazing land when she turned eighteen, but she held onto the house and the surrounding few hectares as a piece of family history, even though she was already planning to live and work permanently in Europe or the States... In fact the last time she was in New Zealand was when she had finally decided it was time to sell The Pines. What a coincidence that you should turn out to be the buyer, Mr Tyler!'

Oh, God, she was babbling. She never babbled! She could see the glazed look of boredom on Heather Morgan's face and her father's impatient glance at his wristwatch. Meanwhile, the object of her gushing lecture stood like a towering totem pole...rigid, aloof and aggressively unyielding, his rough-hewn face carved into blunt lines of cynical rejection.

It had been more or less from that point on that she had given up expecting any positive support from Scott Tyler. The best she had hoped for was that his professionalism would compel him to at least give her a fair hearing. The trouble was that she had found herself picking up his tension like a tuning fork. He only had to be in the same room and she could feel herself vibrate with awareness, and even when she wasn't looking directly at him he loomed larger than life in her mind, confusing her and making her say or do foolish things. But that didn't mean she was going to lie down and let him walk all over her. It only made her more determined to fight back.

Anya slid down into the bath until the fragrant waves lapped the point of her chin, soaking the tendrils of hair that had steamed free of the knot on the top of her head.

Scott Tyler was a menace. Now he had even followed her into the sanctuary of sanctuaries, her bath. Looking down through the misty water, she could see her small bobbing breasts and boyish hips, so different from the statuesque curves that Heather Morgan flaunted around society on the arm of her rugged consort. Of course, Tank Tyler would probably need a well-built, boldly aggressive man-eater to slake his vile lust upon, she brooded darkly, for he would squash any woman of a more delicate and petite construction.

How had he put it last night?

I'm...considerably more demanding than your average randy teenager.

She could just imagine what kind of demands he had been talking about...

A tiny shiver rippled across the surface of the water and she sank a little deeper, letting it creep as far as her lower lip.

He was probably an arrogant, clumsy oaf in bed, she ordered herself to believe, with no appreciation of the finer nuances of making love. Quantity rather than quality. Dominating and selfish. Impatient.

She closed her eyes, trying to mine her imagination for more scathing criticisms, but instead her treacherous mind presented her with a vivid picture of Scott Tyler in the process of proving his oafishness, his glossy olive skin glistening with a bloom of moisture, his hard muscles flexing and rippling as he moved over the woman pinned beneath his pistoning hips, his blue eyes burning down into hers with reckless desire. He had dark hair on his wrists and a heavy beard growth so her inspired imagination painted a thick pelt of soft hair on his sleek and shining chest, that teased at her breasts with each thrust of his—

Aaaarghh! Anya sat up choking and spluttering, groping for the towel at the side of the bath, coughing up the water that had rushed up her nose as her boneless body had slipped beneath the sensuously rocking surface.

Anya scrubbed at her blotchy face, horrified at the dangerous byway down which her thoughts had drifted. The last thing she wanted to do was start having hot and heavy fantasies about Scott Tyler. As if she wasn't self-conscious enough around him already! She looked down in dismay at her peaked breasts, knowing that this time she didn't have the excuse of a cold draught to explain her body's aching arousal.

Dammit!

She snatched up her loofah and soap and began scrubbing mercilessly at her skin, trying to scour away her sins. So much for her nice, soothing, revitalising bath. She was revitalized, all right, but in a most unwelcome way.

She ducked back under the water to rinse off the soap, deciding to follow up with a brisk, cool shower to wash her hair. As she resurfaced, the water in her ears hummed, and she groaned as she realised that it was the telephone ringing in the kitchen. She debated leaving it, but then considered that in view of the upheavals that had occurred it might be wise to answer it.

Her damp body wrapped in the plush white towelling designer robe that had been a birthday present from her luxury-loving parents in New York, Anya padded into the kitchen, releasing her waist-length hair from its top-knot and blotting at the dripping mass with a towel, half hoping the electronic burr would stop before she got there, but the caller was persistent—rather ominously so, she feared.

Taking a deep breath, she picked up the receiver in a tense grip.

'Anya? For God's sake, what took you so long to answer? How far away could you be in that tiny little shoebox you call a house? Why on earth don't you get a cell-phone like mine, or at least a cordless that you can carry around with you?'

Anya's fingers relaxed at the sound of the irritated greeting. 'Kate? Good heavens, I was just thinking about you,' she said, sternly censoring the last few minutes of her bath.

'Were you, sweetie? I hope that means that you've got some good news for me at long last.'

She might have known that her cousin wouldn't ring for just a chat. 'Well, uh—'

But Kate hadn't finished. 'You know, I wouldn't have to phone if you would just use your computer more often—you know I'm constantly bouncing all over the place and sometimes don't pick up my snail mail for weeks. Didn't you read the e-mail I sent you last week?'

Typical of Kate to expect a rapid reply when she herself was notorious for her time-lagged answers.

'Actually, I've been away—'

'Just a moment!' Anya heard a hand cover the mouthpiece at the other end and quietly resumed mopping her hair, squeezing out the shaped layers which framed her face before rolling up the sodden length in the towel and securing it round her head. She could hear echoing noises and a muffled conversation in French being carried on at the other end, with a good peppering of Gallic expletives.

'Sorry, Annie,' Kate came back on, 'but I'm at Charles de Gaulle on my way to New York and some petty tyrant is trying to tell me that one of my bags is overweight for the baggage handlers. If the hotel chauffeur could handle it why not them? Are they all wimps? Why do I fly business class if not to avoid stupid hassles like this?'

Anya waited patiently, knowing it was pointless to offer either advice or sympathy, for it would undoubtedly be taken as criticism or unwelcome interference. Just as pointless to remind Kate how much she disliked being called 'Annie'.

She stretched the telephone cord to enable her to reach the fridge and take out the bottle of white wine lying on the bottom shelf. She had the feeling she might need a glass before the conversation was through.

'So, have you managed to get yourself invited over to the old homestead, yet?' Kate returned abruptly to the purpose of her call when she had vented enough of her spleen.

'Well, no, not really—' Anya didn't think she could count last night's gate-crashing episode.

'Why not, for God's sake? You've been in Riverview for four months; you must be part of the local scenery by now. Can't you casually wander over and say you want to look around the place you used to visit as a kid…maybe spin a sob story about a pilgrimage to The Pines in memory of your dear, departed Aunty Mary and Uncle Fred?'

'No, I couldn't,' said Anya, irritated by the flippancy of the last remark. She couldn't imagine any sufficiently *casual* way to go knocking on Scott Tyler's door. Especially now!

She extracted the cork from the bottle with a sharp tug. 'It isn't that simple. I told you—Mr Tyler and I don't get on very well…'

That had to be the most masterly understatement of all time.

'I know you did.' Kate had been oddly complacent about the fact, emboldened rather than discouraged. 'He's too rough around the edges for someone like you. He'd eat you up in a minute. But you're doing this for me, not for him. It's not as if I ask you for many favours, sweetie…'

Nor I of you, thought Anya with a rare stab of bitterness, pouring a healthy slug of wine into her glass.

Kate had been disparaging when a pained Martha and Charles Adams had passed on the news that their daughter had taken the backward career-step of moving to a 'down-market' school and had bought some kind of 'tumbledown' cottage in Riverview. But a month ago she had rung up out of the blue, telling Anya that since she was conveniently to hand, perhaps she wouldn't mind acting for her on a matter of great personal delicacy.

Anya's extreme reluctance on learning what the favour entailed had been tantamount to an outright refusal, but Kate had never been one to let such trifles get in her way.

Kate had been staying at The Pines while the sale was being finalised and when she had left for the last time—in a mad rush because of an unexpected offer of a series of concerts in eastern Europe, she'd said, to excuse her forgetfulness—she had overlooked the bundle of personal belongings and keepsakes which she had temporarily moved up to a corner of the attic, out of the way of the commercial cleaners who had been buffing up the house for its new owner. Now a New Zealand magazine writer had begun work on an in-depth cover article about Kate and was sniffing around for interesting revelations, and Kate wanted to retrieve the journals and papers she had left behind, preferably without alerting anyone to the fact that they existed.

'Anyway, even if I *did* manage to get myself invited for a look around the house—I'd be unlikely to be allowed to poke around on my own, would I?' Anya protested.

'You're a history freak—attics are history. There was loads of other boring old junk up there. You could ask to see it because you're writing something about the early inhabitants of the area—appeal to his civic pride. Or, better still, do it when there are too many other people around for anyone to notice what you're up to,' advised Kate. 'Doesn't Scott Tyler ever throw parties?'

Anya shuddered and took a hasty sip of wine. 'Of course he does—but I'm not on his guest list. We don't move in the same social circles, Kate—'

'You make it sound like the Royal Enclosure at Ascot.'

Kate said scathingly. 'He's a *lawyer*, not the Prince of Wales. Stop being so defeatist. Try dating someone who *is* on his guest list. I'm not asking you to *steal* anything from him, you know. Just retrieve a few measly papers. Those journals and letters are *mine*—they're in my handwriting, for goodness' sake—'

'So why don't you simply call him yourself and explain you want your trunk back, instead of dragging me into it?' snapped Anya.

She had to wait while another bout of muffled French fisticuffs was exchanged.

'Do we have to go through this all over again?' Kate came back in an emphatically lowered voice. 'You *know* why—because there's some compromising stuff in there that I don't want to entrust to a—to a stranger. Very, *very* personal information that I really, *really* don't want anyone to see.'

Anya had never heard her cousin sounding so near to desperate.

'If I asked Tyler to send me the trunk he's not just going to take my word for it that it's mine, after all this time. He's going to want to go through everything with a fine-tooth comb to make sure that he's not sending me anything that he can legally assert ownership to as part of the goods and chattels of the house. He'll assume I'm trying to rip him off. You should have seen the way he went over the contract the real estate agent drew up. Believe me, he's the paranoid, suspicious type...'

Didn't Anya know it! Unfortunately she also knew exactly how desperate one could feel at the thought of Scott Tyler possessing compromising information about you in his hands.

'What makes you think everything is still where you left it?' she asked weakly.

'Because if he'd already come across it I would have heard about it, believe me,' came the grim reply. 'He would have taken great delight in letting me know...'

That struck a sour note and Anya frowned. 'Kate?'

'Anya, stop arguing about it and have a go, will you? For me? If I hadn't let slip to that wretched journalist that I didn't have any photos of myself as a kid because I'd left Mum's old collection of family photos and my school certificates and workbooks at The Pines, I might let sleeping dogs lie. But I just *know* he's going to go there and ask Tyler about it, then the fat will really be in the fire!'

'Why don't you ask him not to, then?'

'Because he's a journalist, stupid—that would be like a red rag to a bull. He could make a mint on some of the things in my old diaries. I have met a lot of famous people, you know, through your parents and when I was at Juilliard, and on tours...'

Anya had hair-raising visions of what Kate might have got up to with said famous people. She knew her cousin had been sexually active from a young age and saw nothing wrong with indulging her strong sensual appetites.

'I can't promise anything,' Anya said stubbornly, pursuing a rising suspicion of her own. 'And I'm not going to try until you tell me the *real* reason why you won't approach Mr Tyler yourself.'

'Oh, for God's sake!' Kate's stentorian breathing crackled into the phone. 'OK, OK. If you must know, he told me he didn't like classical music and I called him an ignorant, un-cultured barbarian...amongst a lot of other things. You know what I'm like when I'm in a temper. Fortunately, this was *after* we had both signed on the dotted line and I had his cash in the bank. Oh, and maybe after I'd gone he might have discovered that there were a few icky little drainage problems that I never got round to mentioning...'

'Oh, *Kate!*' She had ever been one to ignore life's 'icky' problems in favour of her own comfort.

'*Caveat emptor*, sweetie. I was dead keen on a quick sale and he knew he was buying an old house. So you see, the man would leap at the chance to do me a bad turn on his doorstep. That's why I know he hasn't found anything—yet. He'd love to see me strung up in the press. He'd consider it rough justice, the perfect revenge for my tromping all over his precious ego…'

That explained a lot. Almost everything, in fact. Now Anya knew what had triggered his inexplicable prejudice at their first meeting. It had been the thought of Kate herself, not Anya's feeble attempt to scrape an acquaintance, which had been the cause of his jaundiced reaction. She wished that she had pinned her elusive cousin down sooner; it might have saved Anya a lot of soul-searching.

'Look, I have to go,' Kate agitated, the broadcast chatter in the background almost drowning out her voice. 'This, this—*cochon*!—is insisting I repack my case and my flight's almost due to go. E-mail me and let me know how you get on. And do it *soon*, there's a sweetie…'

'But—'

Anya found herself protesting to empty air. Fretting over the call, she didn't linger in the shower, blow-drying her fine hair until the pale strands fanned like polished silk over her shoulders before drinking more of the wine than the tuna salad could soak up. After putting George out to prowl his nocturnal haunts, she sludged in front of a television reality show busting people in the process of committing shameful acts instead of stimulating her intellect with Bach and books, and ended up going to bed in a mood of belligerent depression.

It rained overnight, but by mid-morning the sky was clear again and the sun beamed down on the refreshed countryside. Kate had planned a leisurely lie-in to make up for all the early starts at camp, but her eyes snapped open not long after dawn and she found it impossible to wallow in her inactivity for long. She bounced out of bed, brimming with restless energy, and had done all her catch-up housework by breakfast. After her cup of tea and boiled egg she had intended to work off enough of her tension in the garden to enable her to settle down to the essay she was writing for her post-graduate history paper.

Instead she found herself striding across rain-dewed fields in the direction of The Pines, fuming over the flat battery which had trapped her car in the garage. The local mechanic was out fixing a tractor and wouldn't be able to fetch her a new one until some time that afternoon. Anya couldn't wait that long.

At least the fifteen-minute short-cut across the fenced paddocks would get her to her destination more quickly than trudging along the uneven verge of the winding road. And she didn't want to risk meeting Mark if he was driving out to meet her.

Thank goodness Liz Crawford had rung with a sympathetic warning. Mark Ransom's secretary was the first real friend that Anya had made at the college, and as the headmaster's assistant she had been well-placed to offer helpful tips on how the various school systems worked, and who to seek out for advice and who to avoid amongst the other staff. The two women often lunched together at the shopping mall across the road from the school and Liz had been the first to know, and cheerfully approve, when Anya and Mark had started tentatively dating.

'Anya? I thought I should warn you—Mark apparently received a phone call at home last night...' Liz had paused with rather ominous nervousness '...from Scott Tyler.'

'Oh, no!' Anya closed her stricken eyes. She couldn't believe he had done this to her. And now she had to wonder whether he had an ulterior motive for his vindictiveness. Was he punishing her for something she couldn't help—being Kate's cousin? Why did she feel such a terrible sense of betrayal?

'Do you know what it's all about?' Liz asked delicately.

'I can guess,' groaned Anya.

'Mark didn't go into details, but it's something to do with you and Sean Monroe at a party at Scott's on Saturday night—'

'Let me guess—I "contributed to the delinquency of a minor",' Anya quoted with crisp sarcasm.

'What? No, there was no mention of *that*—besides, Sean's seventeen, isn't he?' puzzled Liz. 'I think it was more of a general concern about the goings-on and what you were doing there. Unfortunately Mark says he can't *not* officially act on information like that once it's brought to his attention— even though it was done outside official channels. You know how stuffy he can be about rules and regs...'

'It's all rubbish, Liz—' said Anya, and poured out the farcical chain of events into her friendly ear.

'I'm sure you'll get it all sorted out,' Liz chuckled, reacting to the story with a reassuring hilarity.

Why couldn't Scott Tyler have seen the funny side of it instead of going off the deep end? Maybe farces were no more to his taste than classical music.

'What I really rang to tell you was that Mark was all het up about it when he came in this morning—' The school office was kept open during the holiday break to carry on the administrative tasks. '—he said he was coming over to talk to you about it before deciding what action to take. He *was* going to ring, but then he thought it was better to raise the matter face-to-face—you know, to try and keep it informal— so he cancelled his appointments—and I can just see him leaving now from the car park.' Her voice rose and Anya could picture her going on tiptoe in her office to improve her sight line to the school gates.

'Oh, God...' Interview by ambush. Anya could think of nothing worse—except perhaps sitting passively around while waiting for the axe to fall.

'I offered to call to check if you were in, but Mark said

he knew you'd be home because you were planning on working on your university assignment today. He obviously wants
to keep this quiet for now, but he didn't specifically tell me
not to call you, so please act surprised when he knocks on
your door...'

'Thanks, Liz, but I may not be here.' Anya scooped her
car keys off the hook by the phone.

'Why? What are you going to do?'

'Get Scott Tyler to retract!'

As soon as she disconnected the call she flipped through
the telephone book and found the number for S.J. Tyler at
The Pines which she had dialled from the camp. A brief talk
with the housekeeper ascertained that Mr Tyler was working
from home today, rather than at his office, and Anya silently
punched the air. She hadn't looked forward to driving all the
way to the Manukau City Centre in central South Auckland,
where he based his large practice, and then having to run the
gauntlet of curious and obstructive staff to get to the Big
Man himself without an appointment.

The flat battery temporarily checked Anya's momentum,
but not for long. She had already changed out of her jeans
and T-shirt into a morale-boosting suit, but she quickly
swapped it for a cotton-knit top and beige riding pants tucked
into supple calf-length leather boots that weren't afraid of
meeting a few cow-pats.

In one way the strenuous walk was doing her good, she
thought breathlessly now, as she ploughed doggedly through
the lush emerald-green grass, ignoring the bovine curiosity
of the herd of black and white Friesians that grazed across
some of the fields, occasionally ambling across her path. It
was taking the edge off her temper as well as giving her time
to rehearse her opening speech out loud.

It was a pity she didn't get the chance to deliver it.

The short-cut brought her out at the back of The Pines and
she climbed through the last wire fence into the huge yard

dotted with citrus and fruit trees, wincing when her shoulder brushed the top strand of barbed wire and a tiny loop of woven cotton sprouted beside the seam. Weaving her way through the low-hanging trees, Anya was trying to push the stubborn loop back to the underside of the loose weave with her fingernail as she skirted the side of the house and didn't at first notice the black-clad figure clinging to the lacy creeper just beneath the top floor dormer window.

When the dry crack of a breaking twig made her look up, Anya's first foolish thought was that someone *else* was trying to sneak a peek into Scott Tyler's house and had elected to take the direct route. She felt a split-second of envy for their boldness before her social conscience reasserted itself, along with her common sense. A cat-burglar in broad daylight? Then she realised that the figure was moving *away* from the open window, not towards it, down rather than up, trying to crab over towards the narrow drainpipe that ran the down the side of the house. She also saw that the figure was too small to be that of an adult, but unfortunately the sparse upper tendrils of the creeper weren't strong enough to support even the slight weight that was being tested upon them and were sagging dangerously away from the white-painted wall.

Anya's heart leapt into her throat and she opened her mouth to cry out a warning but then realised that a shout might be counter-productive. She saw that the climber had already realised what was happening and was frantically trying to scrabble within reach of the downpipe before the fragile framework collapsed completely.

Anya began running towards the place on the paved pathway that she judged was directly beneath the dangling figure and as she did so there was the flash of a pale face and she recognised the rude young girl with the nosering whom she had encountered on Saturday night. She was looking down over her straining shoulder at the six-metre drop, her mouth and eyes wide with fright.

Anya produced a final burst of speed just as there was a tearing, hissing sound and flimsy creeper gave way at both hand and foot. The girl made a final wild swipe at the drainpipe, her fingernails screeching uselessly across the painted copper, and then she was falling backwards, arms flailing, legs bicycling as she tried to twist her body round and grab at handfuls of the vine to slow herself down. But her momentum was too great and the leaves shredded between her fingers.

'Don't worry, I'll catch you!' cried Anya, her voice dry with fear as she bent her knees and arched her spine, throwing her head back and flinging her arms wide to try and turn herself into a human safety net.

In the last split-second everything seemed to be happening in ultra-slow motion and Anya thought she might actually be able to live up to her words, so it was a brutal shock when the moment of impact exploded on her with stunning force, a sharp knee cannoning into her chest and driving her flat to the ground, and the whole world turning to suffocating black velvet.

CHAPTER FOUR

'OH, HELL, are you all right?'

Anya stirred, realising that the smothering blackness which had enveloped her wasn't unconsciousness, but the black-clad chest of the girl who had landed squarely on top of her and smashed her backwards onto the unyielding ground. Anya spat out a mouthful of acrylic cardigan as the girl scrambled off her in a flurry of curses and knelt anxiously at her heaving sides. 'God, I'm sorry—are you badly hurt?' she asked, her voice thin with fear.

The overhead sun dazzled Anya's eyes, white spots dancing mockingly in her vision as she tried to suck in the breath to answer, but there seemed to be no power in her deflated lungs and she took great, dry, whistling gulps to try and equalise the pressure in her burning chest. Her neck was cricked sideways under the overhanging corner of a low step, the back of her ringing head resting on the damp grass beside the path. As she lay there staring up at the jutting brick she was lucid enough to be thankful that her head had not cracked down on that sharp edge as she fell. It would have been lights out permanently!

'Oh, no—do you think you've broken something?' The girl sprang to her feet, shaken but clearly unhurt, her bright, kohl-lined blue eyes looking huge in her ashen face, and Anya finally managed to pump some air into her abused lungs.

'No—I—don't—think—so,' she managed to croak, mentally blessing the fact that the lawn hadn't been recently mown and the grass beneath her head was thick and springy.

She started to squirm away from that threatening overhang. 'I just—ouch!'

As she moved her arm she felt a fierce jab from her funny bone and the hot sting of scraped skin on her forearm. She flexed cautiously, finding no screaming pain from any of her other limbs, no sickening grate of broken bone, although the ringing in her head made it difficult to concentrate on the messages coming in from the rest of her body. 'I think— I'm OK…just—bit stunned…' she advised threadily.

The girl bent over, her hands on her hips in a pugnacious pose that Anya recognised from their previous encounter. 'That was *such* a dumb thing to do—I could have killed you!'

Anya gaped up at the scowling face framed in its distinctive dye-job, the spikes of gold-tipped black hair standing up in defiance of gravity, the ring in her nose matched by two smaller ones in each ear. The words were spoken in relief rather than anger, she thought, and with a strong Australian twang.

'Stopped—you—hurting yourself,' she panted out in between whistling breaths, in defence of the scolding. At any other time she might have been amused at the role-reversal.

'Yeah, and it's probably going to cost me, big time,' was the disgruntled reply. Anya decided to try and sit up, but the girl dropped onto her skinny haunches and planted a surprisingly strong hand on Anya's collarbone, holding her flat against the uneven bricks. 'No! Don't try and move yet. I'll go and get some help—'

Anya suddenly remembered where she was. 'No, really, I'm OK—' she protested weakly. 'I can feel everything…' She wiggled her toes to prove it.

'Just *wait*!' The young voice, formerly shrill, had now sunk back to its natural husky register and carried an amazing amount of authority for one so young. 'Jeez, lady, don't be in such a hurry. Please—don't try and get up until I get someone to help. I don't want you dying on me. I'm too young to have that on my conscience. I'd be traumatised for life!'

Anya doubted it. Not with that resilient sense of humour. 'You…didn't mean to…do it,' she huffed, gracious to a fault.

'No, well…' The blue eyes sparked with a devilish light that plucked a familiar chord in Anya's mind. 'Be a real mate and hold that thought for me, will you?'

'What—?' But she was already gone, sprinting like a black gazelle towards the back of the house, leaping and hopping from leg to leg as she whipped off her running shoes along the way, dangling them by their laces as she ran. Did she think she was faster in bare feet?

Anya remained spread-eagled on the ground, not because she was following instructions but because she felt slightly giddy when she lifted her head, and her breathing was still catching unpleasantly in her chest. She would get up in slow stages, she decided, carefully straightening in her limbs in preparation to rolling over and pushing up on her knees.

She thought she was starting to hallucinate when she suddenly saw the girl's head and shoulders poke out of the self-same dormer window high up under the gabled roof. The weirdly skewed sense of *déjà vu* was shattered as the girl gave her an encouraging wave and launched into a series of ear-piercing screams. Her head abruptly disappeared back inside the room and Anya was left staring blankly upwards, thinking perhaps she *was* unconscious after all.

To her confused mind it only seemed bare seconds later when the girl came dashing back up to her prone body, this time from the direction of the front of the house and closely trailed by a babble of voices wanting to know what was going on. One of them, deep and resonant, made Anya utter a fatalistic cry of pained frustration.

'What the—?' Scott Tyler's exclamation was cut short as he dropped to his knees beside her, his large hand going to her forehead to brushed away a few crumpled leaves. In his dark trousers and casual open shirt he looked younger and less ruthlessly constrained than he did in his elegant suits.

'What on earth have you done to yourself?' he muttered, running his eyes rapidly over her body, looking for clues. Over his shoulder Anya was dismayed to see the curious faces of Sean and Samantha, his niece and nephew, falling into startled expressions as they realised who it was lying on the path.

'What are you doing here, anyway?' he continued, 'I didn't see your car parked out front.'

'I—I walked over,' she said, watching Sean turn around and hurriedly slope off while his sister craned forward.

'Did you trip and hit your head on the bricks?' he said, sliding his fingers around the back of her skull and feeling for any telltale sponginess.

'No, I—' Anya tried to pull her head away from his touch and saw the young girl looking down at her with pleading eyes, her hands steepled under her chin. '—I fell,' she finished lamely. The girl silently folded her hands to her heart in a mime of swooning gratitude.

'Not watching where you were going?' murmured Scott Tyler, his dark brows drawn together as he bent over her and placed his flattened palms on either side of her neck, making her pulse jerk. Dark hair flopped across his forehead and she could see the pulse jumping at the base of his own throat through his open shirt-collar.

'The bricks on this path *are* very uneven, and the steps do tend to sort of blend in,' chipped in the cause of the accident with inventive flair.

'I was looking up at the house,' Anya said truthfully, gasping as his big hands smoothed over her shoulders and arms, and down her sides, his fingers trailing over the front of her ribs. 'What do you think you're *doing*?' She squirmed as his hands kept going south, moving over her hips and down her legs.

'Stop writhing about,' he growled.

'You're tickling,' she complained, and blushed when his dark lashes flicked up so that he looked directly into her eyes. Could he tell she was lying?

'Well, at least you don't appear to be suffering from any loss of feeling,' he said drily. 'And your colour seems to be coming back.'

'I had the wind knocked out of me, that's all,' she said, putting a hand to her scooped neckline, drawing his attention to her yellow knitted top.

'You look like a wilted buttercup,' he murmured, 'mown down by a summer breeze.'

Anya was flustered by the unexpected whimsicality of his words. Was that a poetical way of saying that she was a weakling? How would *he* fare on being struck by a human cannonball?

'If you move out of the way I'll get up,' she said gruffly.

She began to hoist herself up on her hands but he remained where he was, tilting his head to frown at the scrape on her arm below her bunched sleeve. 'I think it was a little more than a winding, but lying there on the damp ground certainly isn't doing you any good.'

To her shock he slid an arm behind her shoulder blades and one under her knees and stood up in one fluid movement, tipping her high against his chest to readjust his grip under her thighs before he turned and began to retrace his steps, Samantha and the other girl trailing behind him, whispering to each other.

She pushed at his shoulder with a gritty hand, leaving a smudge on the front of his pale blue shirt. 'Put me down…you can't carry me—'

'Why? Don't you think I'm strong enough to handle a fairy-weight like you?'

She could feel the play of muscles across his chest and abdomen and the tensile pull of sinews and tendons in his arms as he moved effortlessly over the ground. He wasn't even breathing hard as he mounted the steps to the open front door. There was no doubting his strength; it was the *handling* part that Anya was worried about...

'I'm perfectly able to walk—'

'But evidently not without falling over.'

He stepped into the hall and there was a muffled giggle behind him. 'You just carried her over the threshold, Uncle Scott,' Samantha Monroe informed him, her bubbly voice pregnant with meaning.

'I doubt Miss Adams is feeling in the least bit bride-like at the moment,' he answered repressively. 'Go and get a bowl of hot water with disinfectant, and some cotton wool swabs would you, Sam?' He raised his voice above the sound of her chunky sandals clattering off across the polished hardwood floor. 'And while you're in the kitchen getting the bowl, ask Mrs Lee to make some tea.'

'That girl has marriage on the brain.' He sounded sorely harassed. 'Her sole aim in life seems to be how to snag herself a boy.'

'Actually, from what I've seen at school, it's the boys who want to snag *her*,' Anya told him. 'Samantha's interest in marriage is probably partly self-defensive. Even fifteen-year-old boys realise that pretty girls who are misty-eyed about marriage are going to be the type to want commitment, and not likely to put out for whoever happens to be that night's date.'

'And people call *me* a cynical manipulator,' he murmured, glancing down at the woman in his arms as if surprised by the rawness of her perception.

She tilted her chin. 'No, do they really?' she marvelled, widening eyes the colour of the sky on a rainy day.

'Cat!' he said, carrying her down the wide hall towards the living rooms. The interior walls and high, moulded plaster ceilings were the colour of whipped cream, and in daylight the impression of lightness and space was markedly different from the effect of the dark-stained panelling and densely-patterned wallpaper that Anya remembered from her childhood, or the garish coloured lights from Saturday night. The rooms off the hallway were carpeted in wheat-coloured wool which from the pristine look of it had been professionally cleaned since the party. She hoped Scott Tyler was making his nephew work off the cost.

'I thought I was a buttercup,' she countered.

'A buttercup doesn't have claws. I trust that this simple act of human kindness *isn't* making you feel bridal?' he enquired mockingly.

'Homicidal, more like,' she said, remembering the purpose of her visit. She kicked with her legs to signal her displeasure. 'You can put me down now.'

'All in good time.'

As they passed the former dining room she saw it was fitted out as an office and next door she caught a glimpse of something that genuinely widened her eyes. 'You have a piano!' she blurted.

His mockery turned sour. 'Why so surprised? Did you think me too great a Philistine to own such an icon of highbrow culture?' He turning into the living room opposite, reading the answer in her all-too-revealing flush. 'Ah, I see...you've been listening to your loose-lipped cousin. Well, of course, it's only there for pretentious show—or thumping out pub songs—whichever you think is the most offensive to good taste.'

Anya stiffened at the implication that she was a cultural snob. 'As a matter of fact, Kate's hardly mentioned you to me at all,' she snapped. And then only in answer to direct questions.

His eyes gleamed as if he read her mind. 'How frustrating for you,' he said with a silky smile, lowering her onto a deep couch upholstered in cream-coloured linen.

She sank back into the plush cushions as he picked up her ankles one by one and calmly unzipped her boots, his hand cupping the backs of her calves as he slid them off her stockinged feet, ignoring her protest that there was no need for her to lie down.

'Humour me,' he said, allowing her to wriggle up so that her back was propped against the arm of the couch. 'I don't want to leave you any excuses to sue.' He turned to accept the steaming bowl that Samantha had carefully carried into the room, along with a plastic box adorned with a red cross.

There was a high-pitched burble and Samantha snatched up the cordless telephone from the coffee table before it could ring a second time, her flawless complexion pinkening as she responded to the voice at the other end, twirling at one lock of golden-blonde hair around a manicured finger as she answered.

'Oh, hi, Bevan...Yes, it's me...Oh, nothing much, just hanging around here...Well, I don't know—Angie and Sara want to go to the beach later...' She wandered out of the room, the little domestic drama eclipsed in her mind by the pressing demands of a teenage social life.

Anya suffered a closer inspection of her minor bumps and grazes and clenched her teeth as they were meticulously bathed clean and the stinging patch on her arm was treated and a small dressing taped into place over the raw skin. She never would have thought that Scott Tyler could be so gentle, she thought, keeping her eyes fixed on his fingers so she didn't have to look at the face so uncomfortably close to her own. Strangely, his deft gentleness made her feel more, rather than less vulnerable to his aggressive personality.

'I'm using hypoallergenic sticking-plaster because I'm guessing that you have very sensitive skin,' he said, pressing down the final piece of tape and running his thumb down the tender, velvety-smooth inside of her arm to linger over the blue veins in her fine-boned wrist.

'Mr Tyler—'

'Miss Adams?' The prim way he said her name made her feel foolish for her attempt to reassert a formal distance between them. 'You'd better call me Scott. A woman should be on first-name terms with the man who carries her over the threshold.'

The threshold of what? she thought darkly and was chagrined when she realised that she had muttered it out loud.

His eyes picked up the blue of his shirt, making their colour more intense than ever. 'I guess that's the lady's choice.' He looked down at her where he touched her. 'I'll bet you bruise very easily—*Anya*.' He broadened the initial 'A', the way it was meant to be pronounced but seldom ever was by anyone outside her family, making it sound seductively foreign.

'Yes, but I heal very quickly, too.' He was stroking tiny circles at the flex-point of her wrist, proving his theory about her sensitivity. Anya could feel the hairs all up her arm rising as if swept by a fine electrical current.

'Then you're a lot more resilient than you look.'

'I thought we were agreed that appearances could be deceptive—*Scott*,' she said, and his fingers tightened briefly on her wrist and then released it to brush the specks of brick dust on her hand.

'I'm surprised you don't have any defensive grazes on your palms. Most people instinctively fling out their hands to try and break a fall...'

Anya's hands had been raised to catch the girl who was now hovering at the other end of the couch, her gaze darting between them, a thoughtful wrinkle forming above the bridge of her strong nose.

'And oddly enough it looks as if you're going to have a bruise here.' He lightly touched the reddened skin over her breast-bone just above the neckline of her top, his eyes puzzled as he traced what he didn't realise to be the outline of a bony knee.

Fortunately the owner of the knee interrupted him before he noticed Anya's spontaneous reaction to his feather-light stroking.

'Aren't you going to ask *me* to do something to help, too?' she said, with a rather challenging look at the man now rising to his feet. 'Or am I surplus to requirements?'

To Anya's surprise he didn't react to the sarcasm with his usual swift retort. He seemed momentarily at a loss, and the pair of them stared at each other across the couch, two sets of blue eyes exchanging a silent message that neither seemed able to interpret. In fact, had Anya been given the choice, she would have picked the youngster as the marginally more confident of the two.

Finally Anya couldn't stand it any longer. 'Perhaps you'd like to see if the tea's ready?' she suggested brightly, swivelling her legs off the couch. 'I could really do with something to drink.'

Scott ran a hand through his hair, suddenly released from his tension. 'Good idea. Could you go and ask Mrs Lee for the tray, and bring it through here? And you may as well take this away,' he added, giving her the bowl of water floating with used swabs. 'Oh, and Miss Adams's boots, too, please, Petra,' he said, picking them up and handing them over. 'Put them out on the shoe stand by the front door.'

'Oh, right! So now I have to do *every*thing,' the girl griped, with a roll of her expressive eyes.

This time Scott grinned, relaxing even further. 'Well, you *did* ask. And I doubt if you were doing it just to be polite, because politeness doesn't seem to be one of your strong points.'

'I can be polite,' came the pert reply.

'Then how about demonstrating your manners now? In spite of the dramatic manner of your meeting, you two haven't yet been introduced.' A furtive glance between the two females was smoothed into polite expectancy on both sides. 'Miss Adams, this is my fourteen-year-old daughter, Petra Conroy—*temporarily* attending Hunua College from the start of the new term. Miss Adams teaches history, Petra.'

'Yeah, so Sam told me. Hi, Miss Adams!'

Petra patently enjoyed the shock in Anya's murmured greeting, giving her a huge grin before strolling out the door. As she stepped into the hallway, Anya realised the reason for her dance to take off her shoes. Her bare feet made no sound on the wooden floor. She would have been silently fleet up the wooden staircase and deliberately rowdy thundering back down. A girl with a great deal of natural wit and cunning, she thought. I wonder where she inherited *that* from?—probably the same person who had given her those forget-me-not eyes.

'You have a daughter?' she couldn't help saying. 'I didn't know you'd ever been m—' she stopped, biting her lip, but he was quick to embarrass her over her near faux pas.

'Married? I haven't. I hope you don't make that conventional assumption about the parents of your pupils at the college; a lot of them come from painfully fragmented backgrounds.'

'I know that.' Anya repudiated the criticism. 'I meant that I hadn't heard that you had children—'

'*A* child, and I don't "have" her. She's lived with her mother in Australia since before she was born,' he said, dropping into the armchair opposite the couch, his outstretched arms dropping over the padded arms, the casual sprawl of his legs a direct counterpoint to her neat, straight-backed, knees-together, ankles-crossed pose.

'Oh,' she said, searching for the proper response to such a statement. 'You must have been quite young yourself when she was born—'

'Eighteen.' He saved her the maths. 'She was conceived

while I was still at school.' His daughter wasn't the only one with a propensity to shock. Anya tried to control her expression but some of her involuntary disapproval must have leaked out because his mouth drooped sardonically. 'And no, I didn't carelessly get my teenage girlfriend pregnant. Lorna was thirty, and she was the one making all the decisions about our relationship, including the one to have and raise a child on her own.'

Anya's mouth fell open and the corner of his mouth ticked up in satisfaction.

'What's the matter? Aren't I conforming to the stereotype image you've created of me?'

She was so stunned she instinctively spoke the truth. 'I...you— I just have difficulty thinking of you as a...a junior partner in any relationship,' she stammered.

'Everyone has to get their experience from somewhere,' he told her, and for one horrible moment she thought he was going to demand to know where she had got hers. She tried not to think about Alistair Grant any more, except in his capacity as her parents' agent. Anyway, she was sure that her limited experience was of no interest to Scott Tyler.

'Are you saying you were a—' Suddenly she realised what she had been going to ask and her whole body suffused with heat. It was no business of hers. How could she even think of asking such an intimate question of a man she barely knew, a man she had come here to angrily confront?

'A virgin?' he said with explicit clarity, relishing the sight of her fiery blush and the embarrassed flutter of her guilty grey eyes. 'Perhaps not physically but emotionally it was certainly a first for me.'

'You were in love with her?'

'I was flattered by the attentions of a very attractive, intelligent, older woman,' he replied with exquisite evasiveness. He might want to slap her in the face with the raw facts of life, but he evidently wasn't prepared to reveal the secrets of his heart.

Anya moistened her dry lips. 'H-have you been able to see your daughter very often?' She ventured onto what she thought was more conventional conversational ground.

'Not since she was a baby. Lorna wanted it that way. She didn't want any financial support and in exchange I agreed not to involve myself in her child's life.' He shrugged at her indrawn breath. 'I was eighteen…what did I know? As Lorna pointed out, I had no money and at least four years of law school ahead of me. I wasn't ready for parenthood—she was…'

There was more to it than that, Anya was sure of it; his whole attitude was simply too nonchalant. 'So what's Petra doing here now? Has something happened to her mother?'

'No. Petra decided that it was time she tracked down her biological father. After an argument with Lorna about it she ran away from home, hopped a plane—booked with her mother's credit card—and turned up on my doorstep last week.'

'Good lord…!' Climbing out of a second-floor window was probably a breeze compared with what she had already risked.

'After some discussion Lorna and I agreed that since Petra felt so strongly about it she should stay here for a few weeks and get to know her paternal relations—as long as she doesn't miss her schooling. History is one of her subjects and since you may find her in one of your classes I thought it might help you to know a bit about her background.'

'Talking about me, Dad?' Petra waltzed in with a laden tray which she set down on the coffee table with a cheerful rattle.

'Who else? You *are* the current hot topic around here,' said her father drily. He looked down at the tray and raised his eyebrows. 'Three cups? Nice try, Petra. If you go back to your room right now we'll only add—' he checked his steel watch '—another half an hour onto your sentence to make up the difference.'

'But Dad—I was rescuing someone. I should get time off for good behaviour!' Petra had the grace to flush when she looked over and saw Anya's lowered brows. 'OK, OK,' she amended hastily. 'But this sucks. All I did was tell Sean what I thought of his brain-dead friends.'

'In language I'm more used to hearing in police holding cells than at my own breakfast table. And throwing food is *completely* unacceptable.' Anya looked at him through her lashes as he was laying down the law, hiding her amusement. He might know nothing about parenthood but he was obviously a fast learner. 'None of us are used to living with each other, but if we act civilised and respect each other's boundaries we can all get along. My house, my rules, Petra—and I don't think a couple of hours of time out is unreasonable punishment. You spend more time than that plugged into the stereo in your room every day. In fact, why don't you take up that book about New Zealand I was going to lend you? In a couple of hours you could learn some of the things you may need to know in school next week. Why don't you pour Miss Adams's tea while I get it?'

There was a small silence after he left the room until Petra rushed into speech.

'Hey, thanks for not dobbing me in!' She picked up the china teapot and poured out two cups, pushing one across the coffee table to Anya and carefully sugaring and stirring the other before positioning it within easy reach from the vacant chair.

Anya watched this small, telling act with a softening heart but she wasn't going to be bamboozled by her emotions.

'I fell for a good con job,' she chided in her cool, clear voice. 'But it won't happen a second time. What you did today wasn't reckless, it was just plain stupid, and really dangerous. The fright your father got when he saw me lying there was *nothing* to the anguish he would have felt if it had been you. You might not have died, but you could have had to live the rest of your life unable to function as an individual, with your father blaming himself for not taking better care of you. If nothing else, at least have consideration for the feelings of others before you give in to your selfish impulses.'

She found herself being regarded with unexpected awe. 'Wow!'

'What?' she demanded.

'Nothing.' The girl shook her head, but then blurted: 'You wouldn't think to look at you but you're real good at making a person feel bad.' Her husky voice dropped into quiet sincerity. 'I was just sneaking out to prove that I could—I won't do it again, I promise.' She pulled a wry face. 'I knew as soon as I got out there that it was a dumb thing to do but I couldn't get back in, so I figured it was better to go down as quick as I could so there was less far to fall. I thought it was too dorky to yell for help. I really am sorry.'

'You had to yell for help anyway,' Anya pointed out.

'Yeah, but it's cool to do it for another person,' the girl pointed out with unarguable truth.

When her father came back with the promised book she was quick to beat a retreat.

'She probably won't even open it,' he grunted, sitting down and reaching for his tea.

'Uh, Petra's already done that for you,' said Anya when he ladled in a another teaspoonful of sugar.

He paused in his stirring. 'Then why didn't you stop me?' he said, irritated.

'I'm sorry my reactions weren't fast enough for you,' she replied astringently. 'I didn't know I was supposed to police the sugar bowl. For all I know you could need all that extra sweetening,' she added in a dulcet tone, taking a sip of her own, unadulterated tea.

He shoved the over-sweetened drink back onto the tray and poured himself another in the spare cup, adding a sparse teaspoon of sugar, then sat back in his chair and regarded her with a threatening attentiveness.

'So, to what do I owe the honour of this visit? Or were you simply strolling by and decided to ''trip'' in for a neighbourly chat?' His ironic inflexion stressed the fact that she had never made any such neighbourly gesture before.

'I walked across the fields because my car battery is flat,' she told him, to disabuse him of any notion that she was in the habit of skulking around his property. 'And you must know why I've come!'

'Must I?' His eyes were steady over the rim of his cup.

'Don't play word games with me!' Her fingers tightened on the edges of the delicate bone-china saucer as she forced herself to calm down. 'I'm talking about your phone call last night to Mark Ransom. You made absolutely no effort to contact me to get my side of the story about Saturday night, so I quite naturally assumed that you had got the full truth out of Sean. Now I find out that without even bothering to give me the chance to explain you've complained to the college—'

'Actually, I did try to contact you last night to warn you what I was doing, but I was unable to get through,' he interrupted, taking a fraction of the wind out of her sails. 'And this morning I've been tied up in conference calls...'

Anya had been careless hanging up after Kate's phone call the previous night and hadn't discovered the receiver was still dislodged from the cradle until early this morning. That still didn't excuse what he'd done. She set her tea down on the coffee table with an angry rattle.

'You wanted to warn me that you were going to stab me in the back with unsubstantiated lies? Mark is coming to see me and I don't even know what kind of slanderous allegations he's going to throw at me!' She had the satisfaction of seeing him frown. 'What exactly did you say to him? Do you have *any* idea what you've *done*?'

'Calm down…'

'*Calm down?*' She was outraged. 'This is my career we're talking about!'

He waved a dismissive hand. 'I know *exactly* what I've done. And I haven't made any allegations or complaints about you or your conduct. I merely informed Ransom—*as a friendly courtesy*—that there was an unauthorised party here on Saturday night and a lot of kids from the school were here with illicit alcohol and that you also were here at one point, collecting some partygoers—'

'—and prancing around in my underwear,' she finished his sentence bitterly.

He kept his gravelly voice even. 'I didn't mention your state of dress—or lack of it. I was purposefully vague. Ransom knows you, you're friends—he's not going to automatically assume the worst.' As *he* had! 'I told him that Sean was being appropriately punished—fortunately his memory of the evening is pretty much a total blur—'

'Fortunately for *Sean*, you mean!'

His mouth thinned but he held onto his patience. 'For *both* of you. The only things Sean recalls of the latter part of the night is you chewing him out for what was going on, and him throwing up. After that everything's a blank. He doesn't even remember *me* arriving on the scene, let alone what he said to me, or what you were or weren't wearing at the time…'

Anya felt a brief pang of dizzy relief. 'Then why on earth did you have to go telling tales to Mark?'

'Because word has a way of getting round, and it's easier to attack with the facts than defend against rumours,' he told her, his blue eyes persuasively intent on her stormy face. 'Sean says that the party was supposed to be just for his rugby mates and their girlfriends, but it became an open secret around school and more and more people kept turning up on the night.'

He picked up her cup and handed it back to her, still holding her captive with his compelling gaze, and she automatically began drinking, the hot liquid easing the angry tightness in her throat. 'I had a few calls from concerned parents yesterday about the state their children had arrived home in after what they had been told was an evening of watching videos. The phones have been running hot amongst the kids and before I warned him to keep his mouth shut Sean had already told a few of his mates that you had caught him with ''some rich chick'', and no doubt they told a few of *their* mates, probably embellishing as people tend to do when they're telling a good story. There are probably others, too, who'll remember seeing you when you arrived at the party and start wondering why...'

'Oh, no...' Anya sighed, beginning to perceive the enormity of the problem in which she was entangled.

'Oh, yes. Trust me on this, Anya, it's my own field of expertise: it's always safer to be the source rather than the victim of information. If rumours are flying around, we definitely don't want it to look as if we've tried to cover anything up, because that implies that there's something *worth* covering up in all this. As it is, only you and I know what happened in that bedroom, and as long as we corroborate each other's story there won't be problems about it. I'm sorry I couldn't wait for your prior approval, but it was imperative to make a pre-emptive statement before any whispering campaign got started that could affect you in the classroom, or some parent formally approached the school.'

Trust him? Anya swallowed another mouthful of tea. She supposed she didn't have much choice, and everything he had said *did* seem to make solid sense.

'Well...' Suddenly she realised the most important point she had almost overlooked. She straightened. 'So you now admit I was telling the truth about what happened? That you were wrong about me.'

'You can't blame me for—' He halted as she gave him the haughty-eyebrow routine. He inclined his head. 'On *this* occasion, yes...I was wrong,' he conceded, with an obvious difficulty that made the admission all the sweeter as far as Anya was concerned. He picked up the decorative plate of home baking which had remained ignored on the tray, and offered it as a blatant distraction.

'Biscuit? Mrs Lee has a very light hand with brownies.'

'Thank you.' She took her time selecting one and then continued to press her advantage in the same, insistent tone. 'And, of course, you take back all those terribly insulting things you said to me...'

His eyes narrowed and he put down the plate with a thump, giving her a sharkish smile. 'I'm afraid I'm not prepared to give you a wholesale retraction. Why don't you be a little more specific? You tell me what each insult was, and I'll either agree or disagree to withdraw it.'

And in the process make her repeat every embarrassing one. Anya bit down on her biscuit with unnecessary force and nearly choked on the crumbs that exploded onto her tongue.

He watched her splutter for a moment, her eyes watering as she washed down the crumbs with the dregs of her tea, and leaned forward, his smile shifting into shocking suavity and his voice deepening to a sexy throb. 'I am, of course, deeply sorry to have caused you any degree of discomfort whatsoever and hope that you'll accept my most humble apologies for having the temerity to doubt a lady's word...'

'Oh, very prettily done,' she said, outwardly unimpressed while inside her bones were resonating to the rich vibrancy of his tone. 'A for effort and acting, but you get a definite F in sincerity.'

His suavity was discarded as he burst out laughing. 'You're a hard woman.'

'I'm glad you finally realise it.'

'Then I needn't worry about putting you through this next ordeal, though I think we both understand that it has to be done...'

The 'ordeal' turned out to be an apology from a very sub-dued Sean Monroe who, with his uncle standing with folded arms behind him, trotted out a few stilted words that didn't quite conceal a lingering hint of truculence.

'I don't remember whatever it was I'm supposed to have done, but Uncle Scott said I acted like an obnoxious little kid so I guess I'm sorry for that, and whatever...and thanks for helping me when I was sick...'

Anya didn't prolong his agony, accepting the olive branch with a casualness that she hoped wouldn't leave any lasting feelings of resentment. She could see no hint of a smirk in his brown eyes which would indicate that the blank spots in his memory were anything but genuine.

'Very clever to make him feel he made a fool of himself behaving like a silly little boy instead of a bad, macho stud,' she commented to Scott when his nephew had slouched out. 'Maybe he won't be so keen to let himself get out of control in future.'

'Maybe. He wants to be a professional rugby player and he has talent, but whether he has the long-term application and the temperament, I don't know. His problem is that he enjoys being the sports superstar too much and expects it to earn him special treatment off the rugby field as well.'

He had accompanied her to the door, where she slipped on her boots. 'At the moment he's bitter because I've grounded him for the next three weeks, which means he'll miss the first two weeks of rugby training when he gets back to school. I suppose *you* think I'm being too lenient.'

'Actually I think you're wise not to go overboard,' she

said mildly, perceiving in his acid comment an underlying doubt that appealed for her professional reassurance. 'Except possibly—' she hesitated, then forced herself to confront the worrying issue '—except where drugs are concerned...'

His face took on an expressive grimness. 'Don't worry, he and I have dealt with that as an entirely separate issue. I'm inclined to accept his claim that it was a one-off, because he's obsessive about smoking or anything that might affect his fitness, but it's still something that his parents are going to have to look into when they get back.'

Their new and tentative peace accord was almost breached when Scott refused to let Anya walk back home alone in spite of her insistence that she was perfectly recovered from her small accident. Under the threat that otherwise he would walk her home himself, step-by-step, she found herself bullied into his prowling silver Jaguar, which ate up the distance in no time flat.

Being enclosed in a small space with him heightened her unwilling physical awareness until she was responding to every drawn breath and slight shift of his body, and she began to quietly fret at the thought that he might choose to linger when they arrived at their destination. She couldn't very well refuse to invite him in if he asked, but she knew that once he had been in her home his pervasive image would be even more deeply imprinted on her consciousness.

To her mingled relief and disappointment he merely dropped her at her front gate as she requested, with a glance at his watch and a brief instruction to answer Mark's questions without going into unnecessary detail, and to try to sound casual and amused rather than angry or shocked.

CHAPTER FIVE

'YOU'RE going to *what*?' Anya cried, leaping to her feet in angry disbelief, jarring the two cups of coffee on her small kitchen table.

Mark Ransom held up his hands, surrendering to her vivid shock.

'Look, it's nothing formal, it won't go on your official record or anything—'

'You're *suspending* me!'

'No, no, nothing like that,' he hastened to reassure her, his brown eyes regretful. A thin, wiry man of average height, he didn't make Anya feel small and vulnerable when she stood beside him, like someone else she could name! At thirty-seven he was young to have the headmastership of such a large school and had cultivated a gravity beyond his years. Anya liked him for his seriousness of character and dedication to his students, and when his small kindnesses had begun showing signs of becoming more personal in nature she had been cautiously optimistic about a future relationship.

Until now!

After Scott had dropped her off she had checked her letter box, and although it was too early for the mail she had found a handwritten note from Mark.

Anya, I called while you were out. Couldn't wait. Phone me ASAP on my mobile.

ASAP had been underlined twice, and after she had changed out of her grubby clothing and slipped into a skirt and blouse that covered most of her bumps and scrapes, her response had brought Mark back to her doorstep as soon as he could conclude his lunchtime appointment.

'It's damage control, that's all. I just want you to be prepared if I *do* have to ask you to take a bit of time out over the first few days of term,' he clarified, standing up and smoothing down his tie under his suit jacket in a characteristic gesture of nervous impatience. Since he and Anya had never had a disagreement he was unused to her arguing with his authority. 'But it probably won't come to that, because by the time school goes back this will all have sorted itself out—'

'*Probably?*' Anya said in a frustrated voice, pacing around her small kitchen. 'You said that Sc— Mr Tyler told you it was a private party and I've explained why I went there. I don't see why it has to be made into such a big deal.' She hadn't mentioned Liz's call, or her hasty visit to The Pines that morning, and of course it hadn't occurred to Mark that she might have tried to take the initiative.

Mark ran a hand through his close-cropped sandy hair, looking as harassed as he sounded. 'It won't be if I can help it, Anya, but unfortunately Adrienne Brinkman has already been on the phone to me this morning to quietly warn me that she's had to discipline two Eastbrook girls who said they were taken to a wild party by boys from Hunua's first-fifteen team—'

Anya spun around. 'Those girls were on a *school camp* at the time, but the Hunua kids were on holiday—there's no way the college can be held responsible—'

'Not quite true,' Mark interrupted gloomily. 'I did have one other parent phone me this morning—a regular busybody, as it happens, but this time I'm afraid she has a point. Apparently her son, who came home drunk, found out about the party from the college's Internet bulletin board, so the school *is* involved. We have to find out who hacked in and posted that message, for one thing. And she also wanted to know why, if there was a teacher from the college chaperoning the party, the alcohol wasn't confiscated?'

'But I wasn't *there* to chaperone the party—'

'I know, but this is obviously the kind of thing that's going to bubble up unless we satisfy everyone that the situation is being properly looked into,' said Mark, unknowingly echoing Scott Tyler. 'You know how careful teachers have to be about hints they're leading students astray. It's a question of retaining moral authority…'

Much as she hated to do it, Anya felt driven to play the personal card. 'Surely the fact that *you* can vouch for my integrity must count for a lot? For goodness' sake, Mark, we're going out together—'

'Yes, well—that's actually part of the problem, don't you see?' he said awkwardly. 'If I casually sweep this under the carpet people might think that it's because of our personal relationship. In the circumstances it's very important that I'm *seen* to be acting impartially.' He looked at her from under furrowed brows. 'You *do* understand?'

She was afraid she did. 'Does that mean you won't be picking me up for dinner tonight after all?' she asked drily. All their other dates had been casual, but this time Mark had booked them to dine at the gourmet restaurant of the country hotel on the other side of the Ranges.

He thrust his bunched hands into his hip pockets, looking uncomfortable. 'If you don't mind…I think it's best not to, just at this point in time—don't you think?'

She kept her thoughts to herself, her polite smile pinned firmly into place as she nodded. 'It might look as though we were colluding.'

He looked relieved at her easy agreement. Perhaps after her outburst he had expected her to throw a tantrum.

'Ridiculous, of course, but you know how paranoiac some

people are.' He looked down at the half-finished coffee on the table and Anya could see him already mentally edging towards the door. 'I'll keep you posted but, as I said, I think this will all fizzle out, especially if we divert attention to finding and making an example of this hacker, whoever he or she is...'

At her front step he turned to deliver a last piece of gratuitous advice. 'By the way, it might help if you tried to get on with Scott Tyler instead of being at loggerheads with him all the time. If people know you're feuding with him they might be tempted to wonder if you went to that party *intending* to stir up some trouble for him. I know he gave you a rough ride at your interview but don't be too sensitive about it, that's just his way—I'm sure it was nothing personal. In our own best interests, we need to present a united front on this one.'

Of course, it had to be *her* injured sensitivity and not Scott Tyler's prejudice that was at fault, simmered Anya as she let the door swing closed behind him, tempted to give it a swift kick.

She swept the neglected coffees off the table, dumping the cold liquid down the sink before walking into her cosy living room, her arms wrapped around her waist. So her wonderful new life in the country had hit another hiccup, more serious than some of the others—so what? She would survive, as she had always survived the rough spots in her life.

She looked around at the sunlit room she had sweated to scrape down, paint and paper before she moved in, the second-hand furniture she had stripped, polished and otherwise refurbished to create the warm, natural, lived-in look that she associated with a real home. Nothing to remind her of the soulless modernity of a hotel, or the makeshift clutter of a student flat, or the regimentation of a school boarding house. Everything here was hers and no one else's...except the big chunk of house that was mortgaged to the bank, she amended, and time would correct that unavoidable hitch.

Provided, of course, she could keep up the payments, which were geared high in order to see off the mortgage more quickly. A teacher's salary was nothing spectacular but it was a regular income from doing a job she loved. If her reputation was so damaged that she could no longer find work in her chosen profession she might find herself in much lower-paid work and struggling to make the mortgage payments.

She wasn't going to let that happen!

Spinning around with her fists clenched in determination, Anya looked out through the French doors and saw that Mark hadn't yet left. He was leaning out of the window of his car talking to two people who had walked up the drive as he backed out…Scott Tyler and his daughter, the distinctive silver Jag parked in the street behind them.

She hurried outside, trying not to look self-conscious as both men turned their heads to watch her approach. Had Scott let the cat out of the bag about her visit?

'I was just telling Mark that I thought it was a good idea for you and I to bury the hatchet,' he said before she could open her mouth. 'I wanted to apologise in person for getting you innocently embroiled in my nephew's problems, and my daughter was fascinated to know you were the cousin of a world-renowned classical pianist. Petra takes piano lessons.' He nudged his daughter forward with a large hand.

'I'll leave you to it, then,' said Mark, giving Anya a smug look, as if he had personally conjured up this fortuitous happenstance, along with a subtle jerk of his eyes towards Scott that she supposed was both a warning and encouragement to mend her fences.

Anya was still off balance at the unexpected reference to Kate, and barely noticed Mark drive off.

'What are you *really* doing here?' she asked suspiciously, shading the sun from her eyes with her hand as she looked up at Scott, the neat circular coil of hair on the top of her head glowing like a halo in the bright light.

He seemed to have no problem with the glare, his perceptive eyes studying her tense expression. 'How are you? Have you found any more injuries?'

'No. Is that why you came back—to check I hadn't developed whiplash and decided to sue?'

He sighed. 'It seems to be in danger of developing into a boring habit of mine, producing relatives to deliver their apologies. Go ahead, Petra.' He turned and walked back to his car, where he opened the boot and began to fish inside.

Anya transferred her gaze to his daughter, who shrugged, and gave her a cocky grin. 'Sorry. He found out. I guess I knew he would, but it was worth a try.'

'You confessed or he found out?' She could see Scott coming back up the drive towards them out of the corner of her eye.

'A bit of both, really...'

'I went back to look at the path in case there was a real safety hazard that needed to be tidied up, and noticed all the fallen leaves, and damage to the creeper all the way up to her window,' supplied her father as he rejoined them. 'Since you're an unlikely candidate for a cat-burglar, it didn't take a genius to work out that Petra had decided that a simple closed door was the modern equivalent of Colditz—'

'What's Colditz?'

'A World War II POW prison for chronic escapees, you appallingly ignorant child,' was the drawling reply. 'Haven't you ever studied the World Wars at school?'

'Yeah, but I usually listen to my Discman in the boring classes...you know, run the earphone wire from my bag up under my sleeve and sit with my head propped on my hand—' she flattened her hand over the side of her face and ear.

Anya recognised the characteristic pose and hid a grin while Scott growled, 'Have you made your apology yet?'

'Actually she already did that, back at your house,' Anya said. 'Spontaneously. *Before* your other relative trotted out his rather more forced effort.'

He glowered at her. 'You told me you'd fallen.'

'I did. I just didn't happen to mention it was because Petra landed on top of me.' She could see he was busting to take her to task, but she wasn't going to provide him with any more ammunition. Her eyes fell to the object he was carrying. 'What's that?'

As a distraction for both of them, it did nicely. 'A new battery for your car.' He hefted the weighty cube as if it was a feather. 'I picked it up from the garage for you on the way over.'

She noticed the tools in his other hand. 'Thank you, but I've already arranged for the mechanic to come and put one in,' she said sharply.

'Not any more. I told Harry to cancel the call-out. Why pay for something that you can get done for free?'

She looked dubiously at him, knowing she should be annoyed at his high-handedness, but overcome by curiosity. '*You* know how to change a battery?' He wore the same dark trousers, but had exchanged his shirt for a tight-fitting, v-necked, navy top which was casual yet obviously expensive. He didn't look like someone who spent much time under the hood of a car.

'All men are born knowing basic car maintenance. It's in the genes.' Her contemptuous snort produced a crooked smile. 'In my case, literally. My father was a mechanic until my mother died and he took up boozing as a career; then he relied on me to keep the family crate running.' He began heading for the open doors of her garage. 'Why don't you take Petra inside to entertain you with more of her grovelling while I do the swap...?'

Petra was already heading up the path before he finished speaking and Anya hesitated before darting after him. 'What do I owe you for the battery?' she demanded to know.

'Nothing.'

'Nothing is for nothing,' she pointed out

He stopped and turned in the shadow of the garage. 'My daughter's life—is that *nothing* to you?'

She took a step back at his fierceness. It occurred to her that he'd only known Petra for a week and, although he might have accepted in abstract that he had been a father for the last fourteen years, he had been utterly unprepared for the huge emotional impact she had on him. He was discovering within himself depths of emotion that he hadn't realised existed, or which had been long suppressed in order for him to survive. Even though he had been cynically off-hand in his telling of the circumstances surrounding Petra's birth, Anya had sensed a powerful retroactive resentment of the way he had been totally shut out of his daughter's life. At the time he had been made to feel that he had nothing of value to offer his own child and somewhere deep inside him a little of that fear probably still lurked.

'I only meant that I don't want to be beholden to you—' she said, uneasy with the unwelcome insight.

'Do you think I like feeling indebted to *you*?' he asked tightly, his eyes cut-glass brilliant as they scored her face.

'I don't know,' she said, fighting a sudden light-headedness. 'I don't think you do, either. Since Petra arrived I think you're not quite sure what you're feeling about anything any more.'

'Stop trying to get inside my head,' he growled. 'I'm not one of your students—'

'Thank God!'

'I'm a full-grown man and right now I'm going get my hands filthy doing a man's job, so why don't you run along and flitter about the kitchen or whatever it is prissy ladies do while someone else does their dirty work for them?'

Anya's eyes flashed. 'Why, you sexist pig! I didn't *ask* you to dirty your hands for me.'

'No, you're certainly like your cousin in that respect. Kate never *asked* but she always managed to make it clear what she *expected*, and those expensive hands of hers never had to get soiled because someone else ended up paying for the privilege of meeting those haughty expectations. If she hadn't had the papers to prove it, I never would have believed she'd grown up on a farm.'

She flinched at the accuracy of his vivid word picture. 'My life and expectations are totally different from Kate's, so don't you dare start comparing us!' she said in a voice shaking with repressed anger. 'I may not be able to change a battery, but I can change a tyre and check the oil and water, which is as much as most car owners can do. And I am *not* prissy!' she was unable to resist adding in a fierce hiss.

She knew she had made a mistake when a slow, taunting smile curved his mouth and twin blue devils danced in his eyes as he leaned closer and murmured: 'You always look prissy to me. Even in sexy green underwear with your pretty little breasts begging to be kissed you looked more naughty-but-nice-Miss-Adams than sultry and wicked Miss January. Not that prissy can't be just as much of a turn-on to some men…'

Anya's face was still bright red as she slammed into the house and found Petra flicking through her CD collection in the living room.

'Is something wrong?' Petra looked up at her, the small gold ring in her left nostril glinting as she turned her head.

'Yes! That…that *man*!' Anya's hands clenched and unclenched by her sides.

Petra looked around, alarmed. 'What man?'

'Your *father*!' It was rendered as the grossest of insults.

'Oh.' Petra's blue eyes brightened with curiosity. 'What's the matter? I thought he was doing you a favour.'

Anya breathed carefully through her nose. 'He is. He just doesn't have to be so—' she searched for some relatively innocuous phrase to express her seething annoyance '—so odiously *superior* about it!'

'Well, I guess it's hard for him not to be…him being such a superior kind of guy and all…'

Anya stared at her for a blank moment before she realised she was having her leg gently pulled. 'You know, when you use that sarcastic drawl you sound just like him. You want to be careful; it's not good for someone your age to be too cynical.'

'You really think I sound like him?' Petra asked with a touch too much nonchalance.

'Sometimes. You have his eyes, too. What's your natural hair colour?'

Petra pulled a face. 'Brown. Too ordinary. Mum went spare when I did this—' she tugged at her locks '—but I want to be *different*.'

'I think we can safely agree you've achieved your goal,' Anya told her with a small smile of understanding. 'On the outside, at least.'

'Oh, I feel different on the inside, too.' It was said with a quiet determination that was at odds with her impulsive brashness.

'Different enough to make you want to run away from home?'

She shrugged. 'Mum would never talk to me about Dad. Even my birth certificate didn't have his name on it. I wanted to see him but I knew she wouldn't help, so I looked through her old stuff and found a letter from before I was born. It asked for photos of me as I grew up but she never did send him any—I asked him. When Mum makes up her mind about something that's it—you can't get her to change it. Once I had his name it was easy to track him down on the Net and find out that he wasn't some sleazebag of a loser that I was worried he might be—did you know that his law practice even has its own website? I didn't let him know I was coming because he might have got Mum to stop me. I figured once I was here he'd *have* to see me, even if just to get rid of me, but it turned out that he'd wanted to meet me, too…'

'You still took some pretty horrifying chances. Lawyers can be sleazebags too, you know. You could have just written him a letter—'

'And risk it being binned or waiting ages for a reply, or Mum finding out? I had to see him *now*.' Petra modified her urgent tone with a quick grin, 'Before I started having a serious identity crisis that could screw up my entire adulthood. I'm glad he didn't freak out on me or anything—he's a bit heavy-handed with the new Dad thing but otherwise he's real cool, don't you think?—and pretty hunky for an old guy.'

'He's not old,' responded Anya automatically.

Petra gave her a knowing look. 'So you think he's *young* and hunky?'

Anya wasn't falling into that sly trap. 'I try not to think about him at all,' she said. 'Do you want to put one of those on?' She pointed to the CDs.

Petra accepted the change of subject with a shrug. 'I was wondering whether I could borrow these four of Kate Carlyle's. Dad said she's your cousin—does that mean you get freebies?'

Anya laughed. 'I did when Kate first started recording but now she's become so blasé she doesn't usually bother to send them to me any more.'

'Bummer. So most of these—' she ran her fingers over the rack '—you had to go out and buy them full-price like everyone else?'

'Well, yes. But I do get lots of free opera recordings from my parents—see.' She showed her the tapes and CDs.

Actually it was Alistair Grant who despatched them to her, usually without an enclosure. 'My mother is a guest soprano at leading opera houses all over the States and my father travels too, as a conductor.'

'Wow, so music was real important in your family. I bet you got all the music lessons you wanted from the time you were little.'

'The trouble was I *didn't* want them,' she admitted ruefully. 'I showed no musical aptitude whatsoever, thereby convincing my parents they had a changeling in the nest. I would have sacrificed all my lessons for a bit more of their personal attention. Fortunately for their hopes of a musical dynasty, Kate came to live with us and showed herself to be such a piano prodigy it took all the heat off me.' Petra was looking at her as if she couldn't believe her pierced ears. 'I take it you're enjoying *your* piano lessons?'

Petra's face closed up. 'Yeah, but Dad only pays for one hour a week so I babysit to earn the money to pay for an extra lesson.'

'Your *father* pays?' Anya was taken aback. 'But— I thought that there wasn't any contact between Scott and your mother?'

'Not *Scott*. My *other* Dad—Ken—who's married to Mum.'

'I didn't realise your mother was married,' she murmured, wondering uneasily if that had been the case at the time of her affair with Scott.

'Yeah, they just had their tenth anniversary last week,' said Petra, banishing the disturbing spectre of adultery. 'I've got two little brothers.'

Anya thought she saw the light. 'Is that a problem for you? Ken being their real father but not yours?'

'Nah… Lots of my friends have more than one set of parents. The boys are pests, but they're OK. And Ken's an OK guy—he owns a sports store.' She shrugged. '*I'm* the problem, not them.'

Anya was about to ask what she meant when a prickling of the hairs on the back of her neck made her turn around. Scott was standing inside the door with a stillness that suggested he had been there for some time, listening to their conversation.

'You were quick,' she said, thankful that his eyes were resting on his daughter as she remembered the words he had used to chase her inside.

'I told you I knew what I was doing. Can you show me somewhere I can wash up?' He spread out his oily and grease-grimed hands. He'd pushed his sleeves up past his elbows and she could see a few nicks on his wrists. It hadn't been such a straightforward job after all.

'Of course.' She could have told him where the bathroom was but she was so flustered she led him along the hall and into the green and white bathroom. She indicated the pedestal basin but he was looking around at the deep, claw-footed bath—big enough for two—the extensive collection of ornamental glass containers of bath salts and oils decorating the window sill and the fat, scented wax candles dotted on saucers around the room.

His speculative eyes moved to her warm face, intense masculine curiosity forming in the depths.

'Don't you dare say a word,' she warned him.

'Not even to ask you if you have any chemical cleansing cream?' he asked, with an injured innocence that didn't fool her for a moment. He nodded at the sea-shell of miniature soaps on the pedestal. 'I don't want to besmirch your pretty little soaps, sitting on their dish,' he purred.

...your pretty little breasts, begging to be kissed...

He was deliberately trying to embarrass her all over again.

'I think there's some in here.' Anya reached past him to open the mirrored bathroom cabinet mounted above the basin. He didn't move out of her way, allowing her arm to brush across his chest, nosing with interest into the contents of her cabinet as she looked for the elusive tube of cream.

'Do you mind?' she said, as he tilted his head to read the prescription off a box of pills.

'You can tell a lot about people from their bathrooms,' he mused. 'For instance, you're obviously healthy, except for a little hay fever now and then. You don't like taking pills any longer than is strictly necessary, you prefer the silky-smoothness of a wet shave to the mechanical kind, you're currently celibate, very protective of your delicate skin, and—' this with a provocative glance towards the bath '—you like to keep yourself very, *very* clean.'

Currently celibate? That slyly buried piece of effrontery was obviously based on the absence of any form of contraception in her bathroom cabinet, but it could only be a wild guess because lots of women kept their contraceptives in a bedside drawer, thought Anya. *She* had, during the holiday in New York after her graduation when she had naively believed that Alistair was going to be the love of her life, before Kate had blazed across his firmament and Anya's flattering attentions had suddenly become an embarrassment.

Anya grabbed the cream and slammed the door shut, almost clipping Scott's nose.

'Be careful, I've had that broken once already,' he said, throwing up a protective hand.

'Disgruntled client?' she enquired tartly, unscrewing the lid and handing him the tube.

'Angry father.'

She had been about to leave, but he must have known that she wouldn't be able to resist the tantalising lure of that brief statement.

'You and your father had a physical fight?' Was that how he had got the scar on his mouth?

He dropped the plug into the basin and nudged the hot water tap on with his forearm, vigorously working the non-foaming cream into his oil-streaked palms. '*He* fought—I dodged...most of the time, until I got big enough not to have to run.'

Her heart dropped into her boots and she felt a familiar, helpless anger. 'You were abused as a child?'

He picked up the nail brush in the shape of an iridescent green fish and began to scrub the tips of his fingers. 'Not until my mother died of cancer when I was ten. Dad had a lot of anger inside him after that, and when he got drunk, which was pretty often, he let fly with his fists. He never touched my sister, though—Joanna's always been the spitting image of Mum—and when I got as big as he was he stopped. Never stopped being angry at the world, though.'

'Didn't anyone ever realise that you were being hurt?' asked Anya.

His shoulders moved dismissively. 'I wasn't hurting half as much as he was. At least I had an escape—a future to run towards. He couldn't break free of the past. He was locked into his pain until the day he died.' He pulled the plug and let the dirty water drain away, rinsing the basin and his raw hands under the cold tap.

'I'm sorry...'

'Pity him, not me.' He turned, holding up his dripping hands like a surgeon waiting for a scrub nurse.

Anya hurriedly passed him the sinfully fluffy green bath sheet from the towel rail.

He dried his hands and then lifted the plush pile to his cheek, turning his face inwards to inhale the faint body scent which lingered in the fibres from her bath the night before. 'Mmm...sumptuous. You're really a closet sensualist, aren't you, Miss Adams? Or, should I say, a *bathroom* sensualist?'

'I thought you were going to call me Anya,' she said, choosing to confront the lesser of two evils.

'I've decided I like Miss Adams. It sounds so...'

She knew what he was going to say and her hand flew up

to cover his mouth, trying to smother this latest outrage. 'Don't say it!'

His eyes slitted wickedly above the blade of her hand, accepting her foolish dare.

'Prissy...' The word was muffled, his lips pursing briefly against the centre of her cupped palm in a sibilant kiss.

She removed her hand and scrubbed it down the side of her skirt, but that didn't rid her of the intimate heat of his mouth.

She glowered at him as he threaded the towel neatly back onto the towel rail. 'You needn't do that. It's going straight into the wash, anyhow.'

'Afraid I've contaminated it?' he murmured, pulling his tight sleeves back down to cover his wrists. He noticed a dollop of grease perched near the hem of his shirt where it hugged his broad hips, and pulled out his handkerchief to dab it off, cursing as it smeared deeper into the thin, breathable material.

'That'll probably never come out now,' Anya told him.

He threw his ruined handkerchief into her bathroom bin and took hold of the bottom of the shirt. 'You're an expert on emergency spills. Shall I take it off? Maybe if you run it through the wash for me straight away...' He curled it away from his skin, giving her a teasing flash of a tanned, washboard stomach and a deliciously furry navel.

'I'm not doing your laundry!' she said, backing to the door. 'I presume that's one of the reasons you employ Mrs Lee.'

'It's just an excuse, really. I thought you might welcome the chance to see me half-naked...sort of even the score between us,' he murmured, prowling after her.

Oh, wouldn't he just love to know she had already seen him stark naked in her fantasies in this very room?

'If I want to even the score I'll just sue you for all the pain and suffering you and your family have caused me,' she hit back, aiming deliberately below the belt. 'If I've already lost my job and my reputation I've got nothing to lose by taking you to court, have I? I bet I could gouge enough out of you to keep me in clover for the rest of my life!'

The threat of legal action had a very satisfying effect. The arrogant smile was wiped off his face, his shoulders straightening, eyes narrowing and jaw jutting. As she moved back down the hall he slipped in front of her, his arm shooting out to slam against the opposite wall, barring her way. 'What do you mean, lost your job? What in the hell did Ransom say to you?'

'That I might be suspended from teaching as part of the school's "damage control" if things get messy,' she said.

He swore. 'You're not serious!'

His anger spurred her own. 'Do I *look* as though I'm joking?' She succinctly laid out all Mark's arguments. The sound of Kate playing a Chopin 'Impromptu' had started up in the living room but she still kept her voice low, not wanting Petra to overhear. 'If things do go much further I can probably wave goodbye to my career. An official investigation goes into my teaching record and, even if I'm completely cleared of any wrong-doing, that kind of mud sticks. Even if it *doesn't* get that far I still might find myself struggling to re-establish my credibility—'

His hand fisted against the wall. 'Dammit, why the hell isn't Ransom taking my lead and playing it low-key? I thought you two were supposed to have become *close*—'

'That's why I can't expect any special favours,' she defended Mark, choosing not to make an issue of the insinuating emphasis. 'He has to be above suspicion.'

He made a disparaging sound in his throat. 'Doesn't he realise that it's *his* actions that'll give the thing legs? It'll run all the way to the newspapers if he's not careful.'

'Well, that'll just up the amount of compensatory damages you'll have to pay, won't it? Maybe my neck *is* stiffing up a bit after all. A neck brace has got to be worth a few extra thou.' Anya cupped hand to her nape and flexed her neck with a theatrical little groan.

He dropped his arm. 'Don't issue threats you're not prepared to back up,' he said, his tone containing a little sting of contempt.

'I can back them up and you know it,' she flared. 'You've admitted liability with your apologies. I don't even need a good lawyer to bring a civil suit; I could practically take the case to court myself and win!'

His professional pride recoiled. 'The hell you could!' he exploded quietly. 'I'd eat you for breakfast in any courtroom in the country. You could have the judge in your hip pocket and you still wouldn't be able to screw a red cent out of me.'

'Who's issuing threats now? Did you really think that you could buy me off with a few paltry apologies?'

At first she had merely been taunting, to teach him a lesson, but now Anya wondered whether there wasn't a grain of truth in what she was saying.

His eyes searched hers, an experienced predator looking for the slightest hint of weakness in his prey. 'I thought you didn't want me comparing you to your cousin. You're making it pretty difficult. This is just the kind of stunt I'd expect from her—'

Her steady grey gaze didn't falter. 'Is asking for justice a "stunt" unless *you* happen to be the one doing it?'

'You can dress it up how you like, but this is extortion, pure and simple!'

'I prefer to call it compensation for pain and suffering, both mental and physical—and so will a judge.'

'This is just a bluff,' he guessed shrewdly. 'If it came to the crunch you'd fold. Turn tail and run, like Kate did when things threatened to get sticky. You won't dare take me on. You're bluffing!'

She was amazed and alarmed at her own temerity, but his

assumption that she would never have the guts to stand up for her principles made her dig her heels in. She knew that if she blinked first she could count herself the loser.

'Maybe I am, maybe I'm not.' She folded her arms and raised her eyebrows, the only movement in an otherwise poker face. 'Are you prepared to risk it? The money, the publicity…the implication that your guardianship has been negligent? Or are you willing to settle quietly out of court for an undisclosed sum? Tell me, what's your best offer, Counsellor?'

For a moment she feared he was going to explode, but then the background music paused before the start of Kate's second 'Impromptu' and Scott seemed to use the brief silence to rein himself in and let his astute brain make a lightning reappraisal.

His capitulation, when it came, was calculated and unequivocal.

He folded his arms and raised her another pair of brows.

'OK. Here's the deal—a one-time, non-negotiable, yes-or-no offer: forget suing and I'll use all my personal influence and financial and legal muscle on your behalf to make sure that you emerge from all this with exactly the same reputation, status, job and prospects that you had going in—'

'You think you can do that?'

'Let me finish. If I succeed, you get no cash—apart from the extremely generous rate I'm prepared to pay you for privately tutoring Petra while she's under my roof. This will not only give out the signal that you have my full support and confidence as a teacher, but also help Petra do something about the appalling grades her mother tells me she's been getting. Lorna thinks she needs more individual attention—of the kind that I doubt she'll get in her regular classes at the college—and, Lorna having once been an excellent teacher herself, I'm prepared to take her word for it.'

Anya's head was whirling. 'Your— Petra's mother was a teacher?'

'Oh, haven't I mentioned it?' he said smoothly. 'Her career came to a rather abrupt end when she admitted she'd been having an affair with a senior student who was doing a scholarship year at the private boys' school where she taught. She was allowed to resign rather than being fired, in order to hush it up...'

Anya felt as if she had swallowed a golf ball. 'Are you saying—when you and she...that she was *your teacher*?'

'Maths with Statistics. The lovemaking was strictly extra-curricular. I got ninety-seven per cent in my final exam—to the relief of the school—and she got to have the baby she'd been wanting—which the school never found out about—so I guess you could say it was a mutually beneficial relationship.

'With a precedent like that you can see why I might have overreacted to the circumstances in which I found you and Sean at the party. Women teachers *do* sometimes overstep the moral boundaries, Anya.'

'I—yes, I suppose so...' she faltered, knowing full well that he had blindsided her with his startling revelation in order to soften her up for the kill, and sure enough he moved ruthlessly in.

'So, what's your answer? Do we have a deal?'

'You only mention what happens if you succeed.' She struggled to rise above the turmoil of her emotions. 'What if you fail?'

'If you don't come out of this smelling like a rose, then you can name your own figure.' Her eyes widened at the rashness of his words but he arrogantly disabused her. 'But it's not going to happen. I never fail. Remember that, Anya. When I set out to achieve something, I never give up and I never give in. One way or another I get what I want. So make your choice. Yes or no?'

CHAPTER SIX

'YOU know, if you can express yourself like this, I don't understand why you're getting such low marks in subjects that require essay-writing,' said Anya, laying the handwritten page she had just read beside her on the dappled grass. She leaned back on her hands and studied the girl sprawled on her stomach in front of her. 'Your grammar and punctuation are a bit sloppy but you seem to have bags of creativity.'

'Too much, my teachers say. My ideas are too radical for them, though I don't see why I shouldn't liven up the facts when they get too boring,' Petra replied cheerfully, in between bites at the apple which she had plucked off the tree above them and polished against her ubiquitous black top.

Scott had insisted that the tutoring take place under his own roof, but over the past three days Anya had discovered that the conventional use of table and chairs and structured lessons were not always conducive to Petra's concentration. Sean had been conspicuous by his avoidance, but Samantha had gaggles of friends coming and going and Scott, too, was a powerfully distracting presence. Anya had found it more productive to find a peaceful spot amongst the orchard trees where the casual surroundings caused Petra to relax and open up rather than regard their discussions as a dismal chore.

Every now and then they would see Scott disappear off in his Jag, presumably for court appearances or meetings with clients, but for the most part he seemed to be working out of his study—or *trying* to.

'It's because of me,' Petra had brashly confided on the second day. 'Sam says she hardly used to see him before I came, because he was always at work, but he's sorta trying to hang out around here for my sake. You know—*be there* for me. He bought this *parenting* book, for God's sake—I saw it in his study: *Bringing up a Teenager in the New Millennium* or something equally dorky.' The rolling of her eyes hadn't quite concealed her sneaking satisfaction.

'I don't think I "thrive in a formal classroom setting",' said Petra now, rearing up to hurl her core accurately over the fence into the depths of a bank of low-growing shrubs.

Anya smiled wryly at the direct quotation from one of Petra's report cards. She had said much the same thing to Liz Crawford when she had dropped by the school office to pick up a copy of Petra's timetable and some texts and syllabus information.

'She obviously has intelligence, she just doesn't choose to focus it. Music is the only subject where she appears to score consistently high marks.'

Liz shook her dark curls as she handed over the requested photocopies. 'You're a glutton for punishment. First that camp and now this. I thought you were going to be selfish with the rest of your holiday...work on that essay of yours.'

'I can do that in the mornings—I don't go over to The Pines until after lunch. Anyway, I *am* being selfish. I'm doing this to allay people's fears that I'm *persona non grata* with the board's legal eagle and a bad influence on their kids. It's starting to work, too. You'd be amazed at the number of parents I've run into, or acquaintances who ring me up, and happen to mention that they've heard I'm teaching Scott's daughter—'

'Hah! That's only because they're trying to pump you for information,' was the cynical reply. 'Scott Tyler turning out to have a fourteen-year-old daughter nobody's ever heard of is big news around here. I hope she handles attention well, because she's going to get quite a bit of it on her first few days of school...'

'Oh, I think she'll handle it,' Anya had murmured and,

looking at Petra now, she wondered whether 'craves it' might have been a more accurate description. The girl was certainly no shrinking violet.

She waved away a lazy fruit fly that was trying to land on her bare knee. The Indian summer was still rolling on and she had worn a sleeveless sundress to cope with the heat. 'Maybe if you tried looking on essay-writing in the same way that you look on music—as containing a set of classical conventions that need to be followed in order for you to fully express your ideas in the medium, in a way that your audience can understand and appreciate—'

'OK, OK, I get it,' said Petra, selecting and buffing up another late-season windfall. 'You think I'm paying too much attention to one subject. So does Mum. She knows what I want to be, but she keeps saying I can't put all my eggs in one basket, that I'll need qualifications to fall back on if I can't make it as a musician.' She shrugged her thin shoulders, tipping the apple from hand to hand—drawing attention to the wide span of her palms and long, flexible fingers. 'She and Dad—my other Dad—think that if I cut down on my piano lessons I could put more energy into my other work, but it doesn't work like that.'

She tossed the apple into Anya's lap, amidst the pattern of dark red flowers which decorated her simple shift.

Bingo! thought Anya. Was this part of what had brought her winging across the Tasman Sea? 'It *is* a very tough profession,' she cautioned. 'You need a lot of luck as well as loads of talent and a ton of ruthless ambition.'

'I have talent. I'm ambitious.'

'No kidding?' Anya held up the shiny but misshapen and skin-blemished fruit. 'You're not trying to bribe the teacher into taking sides, are you?'

Petra grinned. 'Would it work?'

Anya crunched into the sweet overripe flesh. 'Not a chance.'

Petra's eyes suddenly brightened and she sat up, then tried to look nonchalant as she waved a casual hand. 'Hi, Dad.'

'Mind if I join you, or am I interrupting the lesson at a critical juncture?' Since Scott was already plunking himself down between them on the grass he considered the question already answered.

'Nope. Miss Adams was just complimenting me on my terrific essay,' said Petra, confident that Anya's mouthful of apple would give her a few moments' grace before the inevitable qualification.

Anya cupped her hand over the spurt of juice which chose just that moment to run down her chin. Unfortunately she had left her handbag in the house and she surreptitiously felt for a spare piece of paper to serve as a napkin.

'Here, allow me.' Scott produced a handkerchief, but instead of passing it to her to use he tilted up her chin with his knuckles, nudged her hand aside and mopped up the glistening moisture himself, paying particular attention to the primly tucked corners of her sticky pink mouth, his eyes sparkling with amusement at her chagrin.

Some of the juice ended up on his fingers and he licked at them unselfconsciously with a limber tongue.

'Mmm, sweet yet tart…just the way I like it,' he approved, his lazy-eyed look making Anya think of everything but apples. She mistrusted him in this kind of whimsical mood. She had earlier seen him in a grey suit, dictating to someone over the speaker phone in his study, but now he was in jeans and a blue Hawaiian shirt—purpose-dressed for lounging out in the open. He hadn't just wandered out here for a passing hello.

'Thank you,' she muttered grudgingly, as she swallowed the rest of her mouthful. She looked down at the apple in her hand, suddenly having lost her appetite.

'Fair exchange.' Scott laid his handkerchief over her sticky hand and took the apple, taking a slow bite from where she had left off. He stretched out on his side, propping his chin on his hand, and Anya hurriedly curled her bare legs the opposite way, tucking the hem of her dress securely around her knees. 'So, what have you two been talking about?' he asked, watching her smooth the dark green fabric down over her slender thighs.

Predictably, Petra chose not to talk about schoolwork. 'Miss Adams has been telling me how she used to come here when she was little and this was her uncle's farm. She got to feed pigs and see them get born, and milk cows with her hands and stuff like that.'

Scott didn't demand to know what that had to do with the fourth-form syllabus. He grinned at Anya from behind his apple.

'I see the sophisticated young Sydney-sider isn't sure whether to be impressed or grossed-out.' He squinted at her as he took another bite and she knew he was going to say something provocative. 'So...you were a pink-cheeked milk-maid before you became a teacher...'

His smile mocked her with the clichéd traditional image of a plump, glowing-skinned young woman of earthy good humour and easy virtue.

'I was only a child at the time, but actually I wouldn't have minded being a farmer,' she reproved him, sprinkling her tacky fingers with water from the bottle which she had lain in the shade of the tree-trunk, and wiping them dry with his handkerchief.

'Or a farmer's wife? Is that why you moved out here to the country, to improve your prospects with the local yeo-manry?'

'I don't happen to see marriage as a valid method of achieving my career goals. I have more respect for the spirit of the institution than that,' she told him, tilting her nose and for once having the luxury of being able to look down on him.

'Huh?' Petra's gold-tipped fringe tickled her wrinkled brow.

'Miss Adams holds to the romantic view—she wants to marry for love, not money,' her father extrapolated. 'Though I suspect, like most people, she might find mutual respect and liking a more durable prospect.'

'That's a very cynical view—'

'As you've pointed out before, I'm a product of my experience—as you're obviously a product of yours. I take it your parents still have a strong marriage...?'

'As far as I'm aware, yes,' she said firmly, wondering if he was going to pick on her privileged background again as he had at her interview. 'They spend a lot of time apart because of the demands of their careers, but it doesn't seem to have weakened their relationship.'

'All that travelling and performing can't have left much time for bringing up a child.'

'Miss Adams had a nanny and tutors and music teachers from when she was a baby 'til she went to boarding school,' supplied Petra eagerly.

'Accelerated learning?' murmured Scott, and Anya gave an involuntary laugh.

'Not in my case. My parents realised pretty quickly that I was never going to set the world on fire with my genius.'

'Did you want to?'

She shook her head. 'No. No...funnily enough I never did. I was shy, and often sick when we were travelling. All the fuss and emotional drama that my parents created wherever they went made me happy to be left in the background. I was glad not to be trotted out to show off my budding accomplishments. The only thing I was any good at was reading, but, as I was telling Petra, if you love books then the world is your oyster.'

'I used to read with a torch under the blankets,' said Scott, and Anya slipped him a surprised smile of fellow-feeling.

'My nannies always used to search my bed before they turned the lights out.'

'You had more than one?'

'Only one at a time. But, as I said, we moved about a lot, and my mother was always very…*particular* about personal staff. They had to have the right vibes. She always seemed to be in the throes of hiring or firing someone.'

'But you didn't bring a nanny whenever you came here?' said Petra, waving at the house.

'No, my aunt and uncle looked after me.'

'And Cousin Kate…' murmured Scott in a neutral voice that made her give him a wary look.

'Cousin Kate soon worked out that I thought it was great fun to do the farm chores that she hated,' she said lightly.

'Don't tell me…she had you whitewashing the picket fence.' Scott surprised her with a rich chuckle, adding to his mystified daughter, 'If you want to know what we're talking about, I suggest you try reading some Mark Twain.' He finished off the apple and tossed the core in the same direction that Petra had chosen, but to a considerably greater distance.

Anya watched with a poignant sense of wistful yearning as he and his daughter talked, fascinated by the mixture of boldness and tentativeness on both sides, the hunger and hesitation that tangled their lines of communication.

A little while later, encouraged by Scott's relaxed responses into further reminiscences about life on the farm and how, a few years after her aunt and uncle's death, she had been happy to come back to boarding school in Auckland while Kate had remained with her parents in New York to continue her intensive music studies, Anya suddenly realised that she had just been the victim of a very subtle form of cross-examination.

'I'm sorry, you shouldn't have let me run on like that,' she said, reaching for a taste from the drink bottle, her dry throat telling her she had been doing far too much talking and too little listening.

'So you and your cousin were sort of born to the wrong set of parents, and then you swapped lives, except that *you* never got to live at Riverview again until now,' Petra worked out.

'You obviously had a far greater sentimental attachment to the farm than Kate,' said Scott quietly. 'It must have been quite a wrench when she sold it, but at least you knew she still owned The Pines up until five years ago.' He sat up to face her with a smooth tightening of his internal muscles, draping one long arm over a bent knee, his other leg still outstretched. 'Did you ever consider the possibility of buying the house yourself when she told you she was putting it on the market?' He watched her grey eyes skate away from his and performed one of the intuitive leaps that made him such a formidable lawyer. 'Or didn't she tell you until after the deed was done?'

Anya shrugged, her finger tracing one of the dark red flowers at the hem of her dress where it was drawn taut across her knees. 'It wasn't as if I could have afforded to pay what she was asking, she knew that—'

'But she was family.' Petra hit the nail on the head. 'Wouldn't she have sold it to you on the cheap or something, if you'd told her you wanted it?'

'It would have saved her several thousand in real estate fees for a start,' commented Scott. 'Did you ever ask her to give you first refusal, or hold the mortgage for you, Anya?'

'It was her inheritance from her parents. I couldn't expect her to forfeit that. At the time she sold she was facing a hefty bill for back taxes; she needed the money up front—'

'You offered what you could, but it wasn't enough,' he guessed shrewdly. 'Wouldn't your parents help you out? They must be loaded.'

'The lifestyle they lead is also extremely expensive to

maintain. I've been self-supporting since I left school and I like it that way. Of course they've paid for trips for me to visit them, and are generous with gifts, but my parents and I inhabit completely separate lives. Anyway, regardless of how much money they have, it's appallingly bad manners to treat one's parents as if they're a bank—' She missed the flash of discomfort on Petra's face, preoccupied as she was with Scott's infuriating expression of knowing sympathy.

'So you asked, but the folks turned you down.'

'Will you stop trying to turn me into Little Orphan Annie?' she said in exasperation, stiffening at the slight hint of sympathy. 'They would have given me the money towards an apartment in the city, but I didn't want that. I'm perfectly happy in the house that I've got! The Pines would have been way too big for me, and I never could have afforded the renovations it obviously needed on top of everything else—'

'So you don't resent me for owning it?'

'That would be as pointless as you resenting me for being related to the person who sold it to you.'

'Touché.' He saluted her with a finger to the centre of his broad temple.

'When you used to stay here, which was your room?' asked Petra, looking up at the wall from which the creeper had already been pruned ruthlessly back to first-floor level.

'The upstairs has changed around since I was here—there were never any *en suite* bathrooms for a start—but Kate and I used to share a corner room where that gable looks out over the back, one with a trapdoor to the attic.'

'Sam's room,' said Scott, saving her from the frisson it would have caused her to know that it was now his.

'This house has an attic?' Petra said. 'Cool! What's up there?'

Anya could feel the blood throb guiltily in her veins. She had tried to push Kate's problem to the back of her mind, but every now and then it loomed oppressively large in her

thoughts. Scott had provided her with both alibi and opportunity when he had invited her to tutor Petra, but the moment
Anya moved to act on her cousin's request she would be
crossing an invisible line, violating a code of ethics that was
integral to her self-respect.

'A lot of dirt, cobwebs and boring old furniture, I expect,'
Scott replied. 'That's all that seemed to be up there when I
did my first tour of inspection and I never bothered to have
it cleaned out. I suppose the builders added a bit of extra
debris of their own.'

A series of high-pitched squeals and boisterous splashing
rose from the other side of the house and Petra heaved a
huge, martyred sigh.

'It sounds as if Sam and her friends are having a good
time in the pool. Why don't you go around and join them?'
suggested Scott.

She had leaped to her feet even before he'd finished his
sentence, but then she hovered briefly, looking at Anya.

'But what about Miss Adams?'

He smiled and a small shiver went up Anya's spine. 'I'll
look after Miss Adams.'

Petra's pang of conscience evaporated on the instant. 'OK.
Thanks, Dad. See ya!'

'See you tomorrow, Petra. And don't forget to read that
biology chapter!' Anya called after her.

'I won't!'

'Will she?' asked Scott settling back. 'Perhaps accidentally
on purpose?'

Anya shook her head. 'She's been pretty good. Once she
sets her mind to something she does it. She's very quick on
the uptake.'

Scott's mouth adopted a wry twist. 'I've noticed.' He
watched his daughter round the corner of the house. 'She's
incredibly sophisticated in some ways and terrifyingly naive
in others. I just don't get why she needs all that defensive

bravado—the black clothes, the hair, the ears, the *nose*, for God's sake. I suppose I should be grateful that she isn't sporting a tongue-stud and tattoo!'

He turned his head and glimpsed the tail end of Anya's secret smile. 'What?'

She shook her head, starting to gather up the books that were scattered on the grass. 'Nothing.'

Her blatant nonchalance made his eyes narrow. 'Yes, it is. You're wearing that damned Mona Lisa look. You know something that I don't. What is it?'

'Mona Lisa?' Anya murmured, her grey eyes wide.

His hand closed around her arm as she reached for a folder, his expression dangerously playful. She had learned to beware that devilish look. 'That enigmatic smile that tiptoes around your mouth when you think you have me at a disadvantage. What aren't you telling me that I ought to know?'

'I really couldn't say—' she began demurely, and then squeaked as he tumbled her backwards onto the grass, pinning her wrists on either side of her head.

'Are you ticklish, Miss Adams?'

A horrified giggle of nervous anticipation bubbled up in her throat as she looked up into his teasing face. 'No!'

He had lowered his hard body to press against her side, and registered her ripple of tension at his question.

'I think you're lying,' he murmured, his eyes insufferably smug. He slowly drew her wrists above her head, gathering them into one of his large hands. The other he allowed to trickle lightly down her ribs. 'Shall we test my theory?'

Anya bit back another betraying giggle. 'This is highly inappropriate behaviour,' she said sternly, as he stilled her squirming by sliding a heavy calf across her ankles.

'Inappropriate to what?' The smell of crushed grass mingled with the spicy scent of warm male skin, overlaid with a tang of sweet apple as his face hovered sinfully close.

'T-to our relationship,' she quavered as his fingertips

stirred against her ribs, and watched as a sultry spark began to smoulder in his blue eyes. Now it was his body that was invaded with tension, chasing out some of the playfulness.

'And what exactly *is* our relationship?' His words whispered across her lips. 'Partners in a hostile deal? Co-conspirators? Combatants? Friends?'

'I—we—' The stirring of his hips against her slender thigh brought her faltering to a stop, her smoky grey eyes filling with a fatal curiosity that was irresistibly alluring to the predatory male who held her captive.

'Perhaps it's time we found out...'

His hand contracted with deliberate intent, surprising a gasp of laughter from her that parted her lips for his sensuous pleasure and he immediately settled in to stake his claim, his hand stroking back up her body to cup the side of her face, guiding her deeper into the kiss, his chest crushing her breasts as he moved over her, slanting his head to seek greater access to her silken surrender.

Anya's fingers curled helplessly into her leashed palms as her curiosity was stunningly satisfied, and then swiftly transmuted into a fierce craving that arched her trembling body against his dominating weight. She murmured under his mouth and he recognised the heated encouragement of a woman desirous of greater pleasures, his nostrils flaring at the piquant scent of her startled arousal, his tongue dipping further into the moist interior, delicately teasing the slick satin walls of her most sensitive inner surfaces, his hand relaxing on her captive wrists, sliding sensuously down her slender bare arms to fold them one by one around his powerful shoulders.

The sun shone through the leafy branches overhead, creating a dancing dazzle against her closed eyelids as Anya sank beneath rippling waves of ever-widening pleasure, utterly open to his demanding passion, her breasts aching as they rubbed against his chest. Her short, sensible nails dug desperately into the back of his polo shirt and he seemed to know instantly what she needed, his big hand seeking out the slight weight of her breast, cupping it through the thin fabric of her dress, his long thumb circling the hardened nipple, teasing at it until her breath sobbed in his mouth and he rewarded her eagerness with a gentle twist of thumb and forefinger that sent a gush of hot pleasure pooling between her thighs.

In spite of her enthralment she felt a tiny nudge of shock at the intensity of her feelings. For the first time in her life she appreciated the validity of the excuse 'swept away by passion'. Her eyes flew open to glimpse his, brilliant with reckless male triumph and a slightly dazed wildness that made her heart melt.

'Scott—'

His hard mouth curved against her lips. 'Hush...I know...it feels good, doesn't it...?' She could taste his rising hunger, hear the husky rasp of his breath, feel the urgent thrust of his desire as he nipped and suckled at her lower lip, his hands moving down to shape her slim hips to his need, his fingers curving into her soft bottom.

It felt more than good. Anya pushed at his shoulders. 'Stop... We can't do this,' she panted.

For a moment she feared that he wasn't going to pay any attention to her protest, but then he rolled off her with a groan, lying flat on his back in the grass, his eyes closed, his chest rising and falling in a shallow, uneven rhythm.

Anya sat up, shakily rearranging her twisted dress and tidying her hair.

'Why don't you take it down?' Scott had opened his eyes and was watching her with unblinking curiosity. 'What's the point of having long hair if you never wear it loose?'

'It's cooler like this,' she said.

'You mean more schoolmarmy. If you think you're turning

me off you're mistaken. Or maybe you're trying to remind me of my historical weakness for schoolteachers?'

His sly reference to Petra's mother made her flush and his chuckle was low and taunting.

'You don't look in the least cool any more. You look deliciously hot and bothered.'

'You shouldn't have grabbed me like that—'

'Why?' He pushed himself up on his hands. 'We both enjoyed it, didn't we? Where's the harm in a couple of adults having a little harmless frolic in the sun?'

Harmless? Anya felt faint.

'You have impressionable teenagers around,' she told him severely. 'What would their parents say if some of them went home and told them that they'd seen you...that you....'

'Were rolling in the grass with some brazen hussy?'

'We're trying to rehabilitate my reputation, not give people even *more* to gossip about,' she reminded him.

He tilted his head. 'Then you shouldn't have kissed me back with such enthusiasm.'

She was stumped for a crushing answer. 'I—you took me by surprise.'

He shouted with laughter. 'I see, so when you're *prepared* to be kissed, you don't kiss back. That must make your dates with Mark Ransom pretty disappointing for the poor guy.'

How he would crow if he knew they had only got as far as a swift peck on the cheek! 'What makes you think that *he* doesn't surprise me?'

He ticked her a lopsided grin. 'He's the boy scout type—he'd make sure you knew what was coming. I bet, to Ransom, every woman's a lady...'

'Whereas to you...?'

'Every lady is a tramp,' he said with typical provocativeness.

'And you have the nerve to wonder that your daughter sets out to shock!' she scoffed, beginning to gather up the books again. 'I hope you weren't including your mother in that crude remark.'

Her pointed barb missed its mark. 'My mother would have laughed if I'd called her a lady,' he told her. 'She was a barmaid—frank and full of beans, always seeing the bright side of life and the best of people. We lived in a pretty tough part of west Auckland and she worked long hours at the pub, but she always managed to find something to laugh about. She brought us up rough but right.'

So that was where his strong sense of justice came from, and his preference for defending the underdog, for taking on cases that other lawyers considered to be lost causes.

'Speaking of rough, are you going to tell me what you were smiling about, or do we get to have another torrid tussle on the grass?' he said, scattering her empathetic thoughts.

Anya sighed, hugging the books defensively to her breast. 'It's fake.'

He looked bewildered. 'What is?'

'Petra's nosering. It's a clip-on.'

'*What?* Are you sure?'

She took advantage of his stunned reaction to rise to her feet, flexing her cramped legs. 'Trust me. I worked at a school where unauthorised body piercings were an expelling offence, whereas jewellery-wearing only merited confiscation. I had a drawerful of the things.'

'The little devil!' He stood up beside her, eyes gleaming with wry admiration. 'She *knew* I was biting my tongue not to criticise it—or her mother for letting her have it done.'

'She's testing you.'

He bent to pick up her water bottle and fell into step beside her as she walked towards the house, intending to collect her handbag which was being looked after by the taciturn Mrs Lee.

'I suppose I lose points for things like sending her to her

room when she's rude to Sean and making her take extra lessons.'

'Actually, I think it makes her feel safe with you. She's obviously used to discipline at home, because she has very good manners when she cares to display them, so when you demand a certain standard from her you're indicating that you care about her future. She's also secretly impressed that you're making the effort to work from home so you can be with her.' She slipped a sideways glance up at him and was startled and amused to see him blushing to the tips of his ears.

'Yes, well...I don't know how much longer I can keep it up,' he gruffed in an attempt to hide his pleasure. 'I can't continue pushing cases off onto my partners, but I don't want her to think that now the novelty of her arrival's worn off I'm abandoning her.'

'I don't think there's any danger of that. She'll be starting school in a few days, and if she's bussing with Sean and Samantha she won't be home herself until half-past four.'

'And then she'll have a couple of hours under your supervision...' he murmured, busily constructing himself a mental timetable. He saw her step falter and gave her a frowning look. 'You agreed to the bargain. Even if everything works out for you as smoothly as I planned, I still expect you to continue with the tutoring. You've seen for yourself how much Petra benefits from individual guidance and you've already established a close rapport. She needs you.'

Petra wasn't the only one. Over the next several days Scott continued to invite himself to join them, and although Anya took care not to be left alone with him again, she soon realised that she was being utilised by both father and daughter as a kind of emotional buffer, a neutral third party through whom they could filter their curiosity about each other without directly confronting their feelings.

On Saturday evening Mark rang Anya just as she was putting the finishing touches to her essay on the cultural impact of taste and consumerism, to tell her that the head of the Information Technology department had tracked down the hacker who had posted the party invitation on the bulletin board. It had turned out to be a student who was already on probation for serious misuse of the school's computer system. A suspension had been handed down and the trouble-making parent's threatening rumbles had been considerably dampened by her son's identification as the purchaser of several bottles of hard liquor for his under-age friends.

Once back at college Anya found that she had to fend off intrusive remarks and irritating jokes from staff and suffer back-chat from more than the usual number of smart-mouthed kids, but by clinging to her usual good-humoured tolerance she rode out the initial flurry of interest and thereafter the fresh scandal of the hockey coach who was having a not-so-discreet affair with the wife of the caretaker took precedence in the collective imagination.

She and Petra adjusted their schedules and for two hours in the early evening, while Sean sweated on his uncle's fitness machine in the pool-room to compensate for his lost rugby training and Samantha breezed through her own homework between phone calls, Anya went over any problems with that day's lessons and helped Petra with her homework. The only thing that stumped Anya was the maths, but fortunately Samantha had an aptitude for the subject and proved willing to revisit some of her previous years' work with her younger cousin. Just before the two hours were up there would be the throaty purr of the Jag in the driveway and Anya would shortly find herself sitting in the living room sipping dry sherry or a frosty lime-and-tonic while Scott nursed a vodka and Petra plied him for the lurid details of his latest case in between swigs of Coke.

Late Friday afternoon, as she was leaving school, Anya

received an unexpected dinner invitation from Mark. Caught off guard, she instinctively demurred but he was flatteringly persistent and, remembering that Petra had said that her father was going out for the evening, Anya suddenly decided to set aside her recent disenchantment with Mark and defiantly enjoy their delayed date.

Deciding to get the day's tutoring over early, so she had plenty of time to get ready, she called in at The Pines on the way home from school instead of popping home first, as she usually did.

Sean answered the door, no longer flinching at the sight of her, and saw her glance at the line of suitcases against the wall. She had forgotten that he and Samantha were due to return home today.

'Mum and Dad flew back from LA last night,' he confirmed. 'Mum's on her way over now, to pick us up.' He wasn't looking overly enthusiastic, probably anticipating his parents' reaction to the reason for his not yet being back at rugby training.

She murmured an appropriate response and he jerked his head in the direction of the closed door along the hall in response to her enquiry about Petra.

'She's in there...banging away at the piano or listening to CDs, I guess. She spends ages shut in there by herself. Screams blue murder if you try to sneak in and listen to her playing,' he groused.

Perhaps Anya's knock was a little soft accidentally on purpose. The sound-proofing of the room was so good she could hear the music only by putting her head close to the panelled wood but when she quietly opened the door the sound of a Bach 'Partita' spilled into her ears in all its exquisite clarity. She stilled when she realised that the superb technical skill and luminous delicacy of emotion wasn't flowing from any stereo speakers but from the young girl seated at the piano, her face intent on her flying fingers.

Anya stood by the partly open door, not moving until the vibrant humour of the final *gigue* faded into silence. She didn't applaud; she was too full of admiration and anger. 'You're good.'

Petra quietly put down the lid of the piano. 'I know.'

Anya moved to sit beside her on the edge of piano stool. 'No, I'm mean *you're good*.' Her voice carried a gravity that extended beyond mere words. 'I may not be able to carry a tune myself but I've lived amongst musicians; I've listened to greatness and I know pure, raw genius when I hear it.' She took the girl's restless hands in hers and looked down sternly into the piquant face. 'Both of us know what it takes to play the way that you do. The dedication it takes, especially in one so young. So what are you doing here, Petra? And I don't mean that stuff you gave your dad about wanting to know the other half of your heritage. What is it that you *really* want from him?'

Petra's grip tightened to the point of pain, her blue eyes dangerously overbright. 'Mum and Dad can't afford for me to go overseas to study. They just haven't got the money—not with Brian and David to provide for, too. Even if I win a scholarship, I'd still need extra money. I could work and save up, but I can't wait that long. I need to go *soon*, Miss Adams. I don't just want to be good, I want to be *great*. But I'm already fourteen; if I'm going to reach my full potential my teachers say I need to start intensive full-time study *now*.'

Petra's face was pale but determined. 'When I found out about my dad—my real dad—I thought he could help me. You know, if he got to know me first, and like me and everything…'

'And then you'd spring a guilt trip on him that he owes you the money because he didn't stick around when you were born,' said Anya, aware that the child had been hoist by her own petard. She might have come looking for a financial backer for her talent, but she had found so much more. And now she was feeling thoroughly torn by her conflicting feelings.

Petra's short nails dug into the backs of Anya's hands. 'I know he was just a kid back then, but he's not any more. In spite of what Mum said, he *wants* to be my dad. He can afford to help me, and I know he would want me to be the best that ever I can be. I *know* he would!'

'Yes, he would,' sighed Anya. 'But, please, for his sake, try and put it to him diplomatically.'

'As soon as I found out that Kate Carlyle was your cousin I knew you'd understand!' Petra burst out, bouncing to her feet. 'You think he should give me the money, too, don't you?'

'For God's sake, don't tell your father that!'

'Don't tell me what?'

Scott, tall and intimidating in a dark pinstriped suit, had slipped in the door. The man had the most incredibly awful timing. He was always turning up when and where Anya least expected him.

Petra grinned, unable to hide her hyped-up state, and Anya knew she was going to blow the whole thing wide open.

'That I came over here to ask you to cough up for me to study at the best music school that I can get to accept me as a student!'

Scott's head whipped around to Anya, still sitting on the piano stool. 'Is this your idea?'

Petra shook her head emphatically, intercepting his steely look. 'Nah, she only listened to me play and realised how good I am.' It was said completely without boastfulness or irony. 'She didn't want me to hurt your feelings—like, make you feel all twisted up that the only reason I wanted to meet you is so that I could screw money out of you.'

'And was it?'

'Well, yeah,' she admitted, lifting her pointed chin. 'But that was before I met you...'

'God knows why, but I find myself understanding that incredible piece of contorted reasoning,' he murmured. 'Ambitious, aren't you?'

Even though he wasn't showing the glimmer of a smile, Petra heard the rueful pride in his voice and her cocky smile returned. 'It's in the genes.'

'Like being cunning and conniving.' He grinned back, and something inside Anya relaxed with a slithery sigh.

He was tough, both inside and out, and, most fortunate of all for Petra, he was a realist and a consummate game-player himself. Conniving and lying he could understand—even respect—if it had an honourable purpose; it was hypocrisy which he despised. And Petra had never pretended to be anything other than what she was—his bold, wilful and outrageously different daughter.

'I only learned to play the piano as an adult, so it's impossible to compare any genetic similarity there. Exactly how much of a prodigy are you?' he quizzed. 'Whenever I suggested you play for me you acted like you weren't in the mood or were too shy...' And he would have been too wary of alienating her to insist, thought Anya, and secretly hurt that his daughter didn't appear to want to share with him the one area in which she was an achiever at school.

'Because that would have given the game away,' Anya told him. 'You would have instantly realised that she was holding out on you. Her sort of talent would turn ''Chopsticks'' into a bravura performance.'

Petra immediately sat down and flipped up the keyboard, producing a sizzling set of variations on the simple, plunking rhythm that made them all laugh. She then segued into some Mozart, and her whole attitude changed, her head drooping, her face becoming tense and absorbed as she concentrated on the moving intensity of the difficult passage.

When she at last folded her hands in her lap, Scott turned

to Anya with a dazed look that reflected her own feelings when she had first heard Petra play.

'What do you think?' he asked thickly.

He already knew. The room was lined with rows of bookcases filled with books, but also an eclectic collection of records, tapes and CDs from country and western to a large block of classical recordings. So either Kate had lied about Scott saying he didn't like classical music...or he had lied to Kate.

'I think you should be proud of her. You have an extremely gifted child.' His blue eyes were glittering as he struggled against an upsurge of emotion, moved not only by the music but by an overflowing sense of paternal pride. 'And I think you and your daughter should talk about what she intends to do with her gift. Alone.'

He and his daughter looked at each other and Anya held her breath. She wasn't sure who moved first, but suddenly Scott and his daughter were hugging each other, and he was pressing a kiss on the top of her ruffled head, his eyes squeezed closed as his arms contracted around her skinny frame, burying her snuffling nose in his jacket. Anya swallowed a lump in her throat as she backed out of the door. This was no time for anything as mundane as schoolwork. It was the first time she had seen the pair of them spontaneously touch each other and knew that another important barrier had been breached—in the politically correct world it had become practically taboo for an older man to show physical affection towards an unrelated female child, and that was how they had both been acting. But now Scott and Petra were truly father and daughter, bonded in trust as well as in blood.

She was wiping the moisture away from the corner of her eyes as she reached the front door and almost cannoned into a big, chestnut-haired woman coming up the front steps.

She knew Joanna Monroe by sight from her volunteer work in the school's tuck shop, but had got the impression

she was a little stand-offish for all her air of bustling con-
geniality so she was taken aback when the woman lifted the
sunglasses from her nose to reveal pale blue eyes and beamed
her a wide, friendly smile.

'Hello, Miss Adams. Or I suppose I should call you Anya
now. Scott told me when I rang last week that you were
helping him sort out his daughter's problems. I must say, I
was as mad as a wet hen when Gary insisted I go and play
corporate wife on his conference trip just when Scott needed
me! Of course, I knew he had a daughter, but none of us
ever expected her to drop in unannounced like this, least of
all Scott! I hope he's not too shell-shocked, poor lamb, what
with my two to look after as well. Not that *they're* likely to
give him much problem, and he does have Mrs Lee here six
days a week—' She had said it all with barely a pause for
breath and as she hesitated to draw her second wind she
noticed Anya's repressed smile.

'What? What did I say? Am I running on like an idiot?—
sorry—I tend to do that. I'm sorry I never said hello to you
before but I didn't realise you and Scott were on such *friendly*
terms.' She gave Anya a disconcerting wink. 'He did try and
act close-mouthed on me but I can always winkle these things
out of him, even though he got rather tangled up in his own
tongue when he talked about you. He said you were infuriating but you made him laugh and I thought *Oh, good*, at
last because it's ages since he's had any real *fun* in his life.
In his job everything is so depressing and serious, and Scott
has such a highly developed sense of humour—well, you'd
know that, wouldn't you? It's just a pity you're related to
that *wretched* woman—sorry, she's your cousin and I know
I shouldn't say that—'

'You mean Kate Carlyle?' interrupted Anya, in fear that
Joanna Monroe was never going to run down.

'Yes, and I know I shouldn't say any more because Scott
will kill me but—well, one minute she's cuddling up to him

all lovey-dovey, and rabbiting on about giving up her career for him and the next—bang! She's gone without a single word. Not even a Dear John letter to tell him why she went, just a note from her agent about a concert booking. She dumped poor Scott two weeks later by e-mail—*e-mail*, can you believe it!'

Anya could, and she couldn't.

There was a pain in her chest so intense she could hardly breathe. Scott and Kate had had an *affair*?

'Are you saying that Scott was *in love* with Kate?'

'Well, I don't know about *in love*. Scott always plays his cards pretty close to his chest. But he must have been fairly deeply involved to be so devastated by her leaving. He virtually stopped dating for a whole *year* afterwards, and since then he's never even come *close* to finding a suitable woman to marry. Sometimes I think he never will...'

CHAPTER SEVEN

'WHAT a coincidence, look who's sitting over by the window—it's Tyler with Heather Morgan. They must have arrived while I was ordering drinks. Why don't I go over and say hello and see if they'd like to come and join us...?'

Anya almost dropped the menu she had been studying, her body stiffening with horror, her eyes rigidly fixed on the man across the table. 'No, Mark, please, I'd rather it was just us— I hardly know Miss Morgan—'

But Mark was already getting to his feet, smiling and nodding in the direction she refused to look. 'It's too late now, they've seen me. Besides, you should see it as a chance to get to know her better. It's good politics to be friendly with people like the Morgans...'

'They're on a date; they'd probably much rather be left alone,' said Anya desperately, but she was talking to thin air as Mark strolled across the busy restaurant to the table where the other couple were being fussed over by the head waiter.

Coincidence? Anya would rather call it horrific bad luck. The old-fashioned pub restaurant was popular with people from Riverview because it was halfway between the town and the motorway which was the main commuter corridor between the city of Auckland and all points south, but she wouldn't have thought it stylish enough for Heather Morgan's tastes. She was certainly among the most smartly dressed, in a glittery red cocktail dress, while her companion—leaning back in his chair to speak to Mark—was more subdued but no less elegant in a dark suit, where most of the other men in the restaurant were in sports jackets or shirtsleeves. His eyes flicked past Mark to capture Anya's un-

127

smiling gaze, and she felt a rush of panic, jerking her eyes back to her menu, her heart thumping uncomfortably in her chest.

She bent her head, staring unseeingly at the ornately printed words, silently cursing herself for her foolish reaction. She should have smiled and coolly inclined her head instead of acting like a frightened ostrich. What she had done had amounted to an outright snub. She didn't dare look up again and almost melted in relief when Mark reappeared, alone.

Relief turned to dismay as he moved around to grasp the back of her chair. 'Come on—Scott's invited us to be *his* guests for the evening. I tried to protest but he insisted—he said their corner table is much better suited to conversation.'

That was what Anya was afraid of! 'But we've already ordered our drinks—' she protested feebly.

'The waiter's sorting that out. He's happy because we're freeing up a table for more customers.'

Anya tried not to resent Mark's guiding hand on her back as she walked towards the flames of hell. He wasn't to know that she was still shell-shocked by Joanna Monroe's devastating revelation. For some reason Joanna had seemed to think that Anya was now part of Scott's intimate inner circle, and naturally assumed that she had known about the turbulent affair.

She stretched a smile across her face as they reached the table, conscious that her unadorned black slip dress with its filmy, beaded overtop was no match for the other woman's dramatic flair, and wished she had worn her hair in a more sophisticated style than the simple French braid that hung down her back. She had always believed that the inner person mattered more than the outer one but it would be nice, just once, to be able to out-dazzle the opposition.

Scott had risen to his feet and she was forced to briefly look him in the eye during the exchange of greetings, pretending not to notice the threatening determination she glimpsed in his studied politeness. His tigerish smile told her he was highly satisfied with the turn of events, while Heather's tight, brief effort suggested that she held the opposite view of the disruption to her evening.

Etiquette demanded that Mark sit next to Heather while Anya sat beside Scott, which at least saved her the nerve-racking prospect of having to converse with him face-to-face, but the table's banquette seats made the brushing of arms and legs inevitable when sharing with a man as tall and broad as Scott, and Anya's nerves soon began to hum at the suspicious frequency with which he was casually rearranging his limbs.

'Having trouble with your contact lenses, or do you need those to read the menu?' drawled Heather, and Kate put a hand up to her face and realised that she was still wearing her driving glasses.

'I use them for long-distance—like when I'm driving.' Annoyed with Mark for not mentioning them before, she quickly whisked them off with fumbling fingers that bounced them onto Scott's bread and butter plate.

'And in the classroom—to keep your eye on the delinquents and troublemakers who always try to hide themselves in the back row,' Mark jokingly reminded her.

'*I* used to sit in the back row,' Scott murmured, picking up the spectacles and folding them up.

'Why am I not surprised?' It came out a little tarter than was strictly polite and was rewarded with instant punishment.

'They must make you look even more like the quintessential schoolmarm,' he said, handing them back for her to stuff in her purse, his eyes wickedly bland as they reminded her of his supposed predilection.

Heather Morgan chuckled sympathetically at what she assumed was a disparaging remark. 'Did you use them to drive here tonight?' Her speculative brown eyes shifted from Anya to Mark. 'I thought you two were here together...?'

'I got called out to a fire alarm at the college, so I wasn't able to pick Anya up as we'd planned,' Mark told her. 'It turned out to be a false alarm, but with vandalism as rife as it is we don't like to take chances, so I got the fire department to do a full check of the premises.'

'We had other plans, too.' The diamonds in her ears glinted as Heather tossed a mildly reproachful look across the table. 'We were supposed to be going to a Law Society dinner in the city but Scott got caught up in some fresh drama with his little daughter that he's not talking about, didn't you, darling?' The clipped consonants indicated a hint of over-strained patience. Anya had already gathered from Petra that the girl's arrival was viewed as a tiresome but temporary blip on Heather Morgan's personal radar. Her condescending in-terest had not endeared her to Petra.

'I did suggest that you could go without me,' drawled Scott, as the waiter served their drinks.

'But of course I wouldn't *hear* of it, even though the din-ner was honouring the achievements of one of my colleagues in the firm,' Heather continued with an attractive little moue of her glossy carmine mouth which emphasised the extent of her self-sacrifice. 'Since I'd skipped lunch in anticipation of a big dinner, Scott decided he'd better feed me at the nearest decent local eatery.' She opened the folder in her hands and studied it with critically raised eyebrows. 'It's quite an ex-tensive menu, but a little on the unimaginative side.'

'It's excellent food, though,' said Mark. 'They have a live band on Friday and Saturday nights, too. Not the head-bashing stuff they have in the public bar, but a good blend of dance music...'

They ordered their meal and Anya, who had not felt much like eating anyway, now found her stomach churning at the thought of anything on the menu. She finally opted for the blandest thing she could find—consommé followed by grilled fish and a green salad.

The talk was blessedly impersonal for a while, with Anya

valiantly keeping up her end of the general conversation in spite of some distracting asides from Scott which were designed to force her to turn her head, or risk seeming spectacularly rude to the man who was paying for her meal. When the wine list arrived and Mark deferred to him as host, Scott consulted Anya's opinion on his choices and she had to confess her ignorance.

'If I like the taste, I'll drink it, but the only thing I really know anything about is champagne—'

'You mean the local bubbly?' Heather interrupted, her voice nasal with disdain. 'They're not allowed to call it champagne any more, it has to be *méthode champenoise*.'

'Oh, I meant Krug and Dom Perignon,' Anya was startled into saying. 'Champagne is the only alcohol my mother ever touches. She says it's good for the throat. Even as a child I was given a small glass and expected to toast her success.'

Scott unwisely chuckled at Heather's ill-concealed chagrin and earned himself a chilly look. He explained about Anya's background, adding several details that he could have gleaned only from Petra. The thought that she was an object of conversation between Scott and his daughter gave her an odd frisson.

'Why didn't you go to an American private school if your parents were living in the States?' Heather wanted to know.

Anya could imagine the supercilious reaction if she said that to her parents she had been a woeful distraction from their joint careers. They'd despaired of what to do with the quiet little cuckoo in their moveable nest, and had been relieved at her naively expressed desire to live in Auckland, 'near where Aunty Mary and Uncle Fred used to live'.

'Because she considers New Zealand her spiritual as well as her birth home.' Scott spoke for her with a lazy blend of amusement and approval which suggested a degree of familiarity that made Heather's face turn even more frosty, and retaliate by shifting the main focus of her attention onto Mark.

Her cold-shouldering had no effect, and instead of competing to recapture her interest, as he was supposed to, Scott was left free to torment Anya with his full awareness. Heather's displeasure became even more pronounced when, over their main course, Mark made a passing remark about the college's reputation for equality and fairness and Scott swiftly took him to task for his lack of recent fairness to Anya, countering every excuse he presented.

'Well, Anya has sure got you on her side,' said Mark ruefully, when Scott had manoeuvred him into admitting and apologising for his over-zealousness.

'Doesn't that present you with rather a conflict of interest—seeing as you're the college's legal representative?' Heather pointed out acidly.

'Naturally I couldn't have advised her myself—but Anya would have had excellent grounds for suing if Mark had suspended her on the speculative fear of a future rumour rather than any eye-witness testimony of wrong-doing...'

The others had finished their mains and Scott watched as Anya pushed the salad around on her plate to disguise the fact she'd hardly touched her food.

He leaned over so that his shoulder touched hers. 'Not hungry?' he asked softly, under cover of the talk on the other side of the table.

'I *was*,' she lied pointedly, in a correspondingly low tone. 'But something in the vicinity seems be turning my stomach.'

Instead of being chastened, he chuckled. 'Let's see if we can't do something to exercise your appetites.' He began to shift across the banquette, nudging her off the bench seat with the hard pressure of his hip and thigh.

'You two carry on with your conversation—Anya and I are just going to try out the band,' he said, and had her in the centre of the small group of slow-dancing couples on the dance floor before she or anyone else had a chance to express an opinion of his manners.

'Your girlfriend is not amused at your behaviour,' said Anya, helpless to prevent her body shivering against his when his arm contracted across her back, enfolding her in the wings of his open jacket, his other hand cupping hers against the smooth weave of his shirt instead of in the correctly polite position. Her head was turned to one side, to prevent her nose being buried in his snowy breast, the top of her head barely reaching his collarbone.

'Then it's as well I'm not her court jester. I'm not any more amused at her mood. And she's hardly a girl,' he said, turning her so that she could no longer see their table, his foot pivoting between hers, his knee briefly kissing the inside of her thigh.

'That's right...your taste runs to older women, doesn't it?' she jabbed breathlessly. 'You're such a champion of the underdog, I suppose you're used to handling bitches.'

To her fury he laughed. 'I think I've got my hands on one right now. And to think I thought you were too soft and tender-hearted. What's got you clawing and biting? Or need I ask? Your cousin is younger than I am but she certainly ranks as a bitch.'

She stiffened in the circle of his arms and the hand on her spine moved, capturing the end of her plait and wrapping it around his wrist so that he could tug her head back and look down into her stormy face. 'I know that my sister, in her inimitable motor-mouthed wisdom, welcomed you into her acquaintance by spilling the beans about Kate and me, so let's stop the sniping and get it out in the open—'

'Oh, so *now* you want to talk about it? Well, maybe I don't!' She jerked her head to try and free her hair, the sharp tugging on her scalp bringing tears to her eyes...or so she wanted to believe as he instantly unwrapped his hand and smoothed the plait down her spine, allowing her the freedom to avert her gaze. She tried to increase the distance between them, but he had reached the limits of his tolerance and bracing herself against his controlling arm merely arched her body into greater intimacy.

'You're angry with me for not telling you?' he said, his eyes on her pale profile. 'I might point out that Kate obviously didn't tell you either.'

He wasn't going to get away with making her sound unreasonable and illogical. She had every right to feel searingly betrayed. She knew exactly why Kate hadn't told her—because it might have made Anya even more reluctant to take any risks on her behalf to know that she was dealing with one of her cousin's ruthlessly discarded lovers.

'Yes, and I'm furious with her, too.'

He had reduced their steps to a bare shuffle, the better to protect the intimacy of their exchange, his head bowed over hers. 'And since she's not here you're going to take it all out on me?'

'Yes!'

'That isn't very fair,' he murmured. 'What happened between Kate and me isn't relevant to this relationship—'

'Isn't *relevant*? You had a love affair with my *cousin* and didn't think it worth *mentioning*?'

'There's a certain etiquette involved in discussing one's past liaisons—particularly when they're with well-known people. When I realised that Kate hadn't told you, I was presented with a dilemma. How could I betray something she clearly wanted held in confidence? Would you respect me if you knew I was the kind of man to kiss and tell?'

'From what your sister told me, it was a hell of a lot more than *kisses*!' hissed Anya, conscious of the relaxed looseness of his body as it teased at her stubborn rigidity.

'It was also five years ago. Well in the past. And I'd prefer it to remain there. I don't make a habit of discussing my past lovers with future partners. That's not my style.'

Future partners? Anya went weak at the knees, telling herself he was just toying with her. She knew she was totally different from the other women he had had in his life. 'And we all know what *your* style is,' she said, catching a glimpse of Heather's haughtily aloof face.

'Oh? What's that?' he asked, again turning her back into the thick of the dancers.

'Sophisticated, successful, beautiful...'

'—and don't forget bitchy,' he had the nerve to tack on with a hint of laughter in his voice, his hand pressing hers into the warmth of his chest, making her aware of the springy cushion of hair under his shirt.

'Elegant women who wouldn't dream of...of—'

'Rolling around on the grass with me under the trees?'

He was definitely laughing at her. Her hand clenched into a fist underneath his palm. 'I bet you didn't roll Kate around on the grass!' she accused raggedly.

'God, no...she hated being ruffled. Your cousin was moonlight, champagne and caviar and silk sheets...everything had to be first class all the way.'

While she was strictly economy, Anya thought bitterly, refusing to acknowledge the sardonic self-contempt that was invested in his words. 'And I bet you loved every minute of it,' she said.

His jaw brushed her brow, his voice unrelenting as he uttered the confidences that she had demanded from him but hadn't really wanted to hear.

'As you say, she's a very beautiful woman, but suffice it to say that I didn't do the chasing. I was single and unencumbered, and I wouldn't have been a man if I hadn't been seduced by her passionate declarations. I admit, I temporarily lost my head. For all of eight weeks she had me convinced I was central to her happiness and I was arrogant enough to actually start believing that she meant it when she said she loved me, that we might be building something special. It was quite a kick in the ego when the attraction didn't last—on *either* side. It was an affair, certainly, but in retrospect I don't think I'd classify it as a *love* affair...

'Five years ago I might have mistaken glister for gold but my tastes have matured since then. Maybe I'm discovering that I prefer to lose my head over the simple pleasures of life—sunlight and laughter, apples and grass, and a pair of eyes as clear and refreshing as a cool drink of water...'

His hand had somehow insinuated itself under the filmy fabric of her little cropped top, his fingertips resting on her silky bare skin above the low-cut back of her dress. Not caressing, or doing anything indecent, just *there*...as seductively enticing as his words.

'You must have been pretty serious about Kate at the time,' she tortured herself. 'Your sister said you didn't date for a *year* afterwards—'

He snorted. 'Jo is a dyed-in-the-wool romantic. It was actually longer than a year. I was building up my practice as fast as I could and at the same time supervising all the renovations being done on The Pines both before and after I moved in. For a long time I simply didn't have the spare energy to devote to a new relationship. My sex drive was sublimated in work. I didn't have *time* for another woman in my life—'

'But now you do,' Anya said tartly, her feminine hackles rising. She stopped moving, glaring up at him. 'Do you know how arrogant that sounds?'

He kept his arm firmly around her, their bodies touching from chest to knee. 'What about you? You obviously haven't had much time for men if you think Mark Ransom is going to make you any kind of decent lover.'

She clenched her teeth. 'There's nothing the matter with Mark!'

'I didn't say there was...only that he's not right for you. He's too conventional. One look at your kinky underwear and he'd be blushing like a vicar instead of ripping it off you.' He grinned at her expression and began dancing again. 'You're a buttoned-up little thing who needs a man who won't be put off by those snooty boarding school manners—'

'And you're a white-collar professional with a big chip on your shoulder!' she snapped, her body unconsciously obeying his lead, moving in perfect unison with his changing step.

'Do you blame me? My one year at private school was an education in the corruption of privilege,' he said, undermining her anger with his sudden gravity. 'Because I was a scholarship boy I was automatically an outsider to the boys who had been there since kindergarten. My language, my mannerisms, my lack of money, my aggressive desire to succeed, they all marked me out as different and threatening to the status quo. And when I found warmth and acceptance in the one place that it seemed to be freely offered, I found that trust was also a flexible commodity. I trusted Lorna when she said she loved me, but she traded on that trust to deny me the true realisation of what it means to be a man.

'I trusted your cousin, too, to be honest about her emotions and open about her intentions, but Kate wasn't capable of that much unselfishness. Her claims of love were just flashy pyrotechnics, full of noise and dazzle but utterly ephemeral. So don't ever think that there's any way that I'd want your cousin back, or confuse you with her...or her with you...'

His words lingered in her head for the entire weekend, during which she cravenly stayed home and gardened. Heather had been sitting in glacial silence by the time they had got back to the table and Anya had quickly invented a headache which Mark had accepted with relief as a reason to excuse themselves from dessert and coffee. Anya had had the feeling that if she hadn't been driving herself she would have had to listen to a lecture all the way home in the car. As it was she had escaped with only an irritated comment that in being submissive to Scott's domination she had only succeeded in being rude to Heather.

Submissive? If only he knew!

She was not feeling at all submissive on Monday afternoon, when the final bell dismissed her last class and Petra bounced into her classroom towing her father.

'Hi, Miss Adams. I hope your headache's better because Dad and I've got a fantastic surprise for you!'

'Oh, really?' said Anya, moving behind her desk, taking off her spectacles and making a business of putting them in their soft leather case in order to avoid Scott's hooded gaze. He doubtless knew very well the reason that she had not tutored Petra over the weekend was because she had not wanted to face him. Her headache had not been organic.

'Yes—look! Dad's got us tickets to go to a concert at the Auckland Town Hall tonight.' Petra released her father's hand to excitedly pull the tickets out of their printed sleeve. 'They've apparently been sold out for *weeks* but Dad managed to get three review seats from a friend at one of the newspapers.' She pushed the tickets across the desk to Anya, pointing out the name of a famous Russian pianist appearing 'For One Night Only'. 'He's playing Beethoven's "Fifth Concerto"—the "Emperor",' she exalted. 'This is just going to be *so* fantastic!'

'Tonight…?' said Anya faintly, folding into the chair behind her desk, frantically trying to think up an excuse.

'You already have a date?' asked Scott, his eyes no longer hooded but blazing with challenge. He was going to pin her to the blackboard behind her if she tried to refuse, she realised.

'Well, no, but…it's a school night,' she faltered, rolling nervously at the fine gold chain exposed by the open collar of her yellow blouse.

'Oh, that's OK, we're not going to be out too late—Dad's booking a hotel suite so we don't have to drive all the way back home tonight.' Petra was almost dancing with glee at the idea. 'We can take everything we'll need for tomorrow and Dad'll drive us home in the morning and drop us right here at school.'

'The perfect plan,' purred Scott, and something in his voice alerted Petra because her face fell with ludicrous speed.

'You're not going to say *no*, are you, Miss Adams? I've never been to a concert where someone famous is playing— just free ones and symphony matinées…'

Anya had picked up a pen from her desk, instinctively trying to retreat behind her professional facade.

'No, Miss Adams is definitely not going to say no,' her father said in that same, silken voice, leaning both hands flat on the edge of her desk. 'She wouldn't *dream* of disappointing you. She's delighted that I'm thoughtful enough to want to ensure that she's bright-eyed and bushy-tailed for school tomorrow. She's going to thank me nicely and say that she feels privileged to be able to attend a concert by a former Tchaikovsky prize-winner in the presence of a *future* Tchaikovsky prize-winner.'

'Oh, *Dad*!'

'Well, if you're sure there's no-one else you'd rather invite,' Anya murmured. 'Someone in the family. Or perhaps Miss Morgan would like to hear the "Emperor"…' she felt driven to suggest.

'Miss *Adams*!' Petra stared at her, eyes rounded in horror at this unthinkable betrayal.

'Miss Morgan thinks the "Emperor" is a giant penguin,' drawled Scott, sending Petra into a fit of hysterically relieved giggles. He leaned further across the desk, his tie brushing Anya's open text-book as his deep voice provided a counterpoint to the high-pitched giggles. 'She also thinks that I no longer fit her profile of a desirable escort. I've apparently changed for the worse since I became an active father—I've become selfish, rude and indifferent to a woman's needs!'

He certainly gave the lie to the first two criticisms that evening as he escorted a lady on each arm into the concert chamber, Petra minus her nosering and wearing a new dress—black of course—bought from a screamingly trendy boutique near the hotel and Anya in a silver lurex top and long black skirt. They had dined at the hotel, Petra in transports of delight at the sight of the luxurious, three-bedroom penthouse suite, confiding that she'd never stayed in a hotel before.

Petra sat between them at the concert, leaning forward in her seat in the centre-front of the circle, her hands gripping the ledge, while Scott lounged back in his seat, his arm extended along the back of her seat towards Anya, occasionally exchanging smiling glances with her behind his daughter's entranced back.

Petra remained utterly still through the entire performance and during the slow movement in B Major Anya even suspected her of holding her breath so as not to make even the slightest sound that would interfere with her blissful appreciation of the adagio. Her expression was filled with such soul-wrenching purity and sublime yearning that Anya felt doubly moved by the music and blinked furiously to dispel the tears in her eyes.

A touch on her shoulder had her turning her head and seeing the corresponding glitter of Scott's eyes as they shared a moment of perfect emotional communion. With his daughter's coming the cynical, hard-bitten lawyer was rediscovering the joys and sorrows of vulnerability, was able to reveal the tenderness and sensitivity which didn't detract from his toughness but merely added depth and breadth to his character. Her heart fisted in her chest. Perhaps what it really meant was that he was opening himself up to love...

The rousing final rondo brought the audience to their feet and Petra clapped and stamped and cried for encores with a glorious abandon that had the people around her laughing indulgently and leaning over to compliment Anya and Scott on their enthusiastic daughter. When Anya blushingly attempted to correct them, Scott swapped seats with Petra and told her not to be silly, and stayed there his arm draped around her for the brilliant short encore that again had Petra shouting herself hoarse.

Outside the Town Hall they strolled across Aotea Square, to a theatre restaurant where they ate a late supper and let Petra begin to wind down from her excitement, her feverish chatter eventually fading into a dream-like contentment.

Back in the hotel suite, Petra yawned her way into her bedroom and re-emerged in the heavy-metal T-shirt that passed for night attire to give Anya an unexpected hug, followed by an exuberant leap into her father's arms. He whirled them both around, turning her babble of thanks into a shower of choked giggles. When he set her down she didn't let him go for a moment, and when she did it was with a fierce kiss and a passionate little speech.

'I know you pretended that you'd wanted to go all along, but you did this for me. I'll never forget that. I'll make you proud of me, Dad, I promise!'

'I already am.' he said gently. 'Let's make a date for the first time you play Carnegie Hall—I'll bring the flowers you bring the piano!'

She laughed, her incipient tears vanishing.

'Go on, sleepy head,' he said. 'To bed—and if I don't hear another peep out of you until morning, I'll let you order breakfast on Room Service!'

After her door had closed behind her he stood still for a moment in the centre of the room, his head bowed, his face pale above his black dinner suit and white silk shirt, his hands flexing at his sides. 'I don't see the point of dwelling on what can't be changed, regrets are so futile—but I hate how much I've missed of her life,' he said hoarsely. 'I hate that I was so ignorant and uncaring that I never got to hold her as a baby or see her first step, or her face the first time she ever touched a piano… And now there's another man whom she obviously loves and is happy to call Dad—her everyday Dad, who's a bigger part of her life than I'll *ever* be…'

'You may have been ignorant; you *weren't* uncaring,' said Anya compassionately. 'Just human. We're all entitled to make mistakes, especially when we're young.'

'Are we?' His shoulders relaxed under the smooth jacket, the jut of his jaw easing as he lifted his head. 'And what heinous mistakes did *you* make when you were young?' It was said in a wry tone that doubted she would have any to confess.

'I fell madly in love with a man whom I thought truly appreciated and accepted the real me. Unfortunately the real me was too boring, both in bed and out, to sustain his interest and he graduated to a very exciting, very public fling with my cousin.'

'Ah.' That rocked him back on his heels, as she had meant it to, but he recovered quickly. 'So you and Kate have issues about men…?' he murmured, walking over to the bar and uncapping a bottle of whisky.

'*An* issue. And we resolved it. I decided Alistair wasn't worth loving after all, and she dumped him.'

He winced. 'Drink?' He tilted the whisky bottle to show her the label and she shook her head.

'I'm still feeling the effects of the Irish coffee I had at supper,' she said, watching him pour two fingers for himself. 'I don't think I can take any more artificial intoxication.'

Scott raised the crystal glass to his mouth, then stopped, looking at her over the rim.

He set the glass back down on the bar behind him. 'You're right—natural intoxication is infinitely more preferable,' he said huskily. 'It gives you a much more sustained high.' He shrugged out of his unbuttoned jacket and stripped off his black tie, tossing them onto the white leather couch. He stretched—a long, slow flex of his big body—and then strolled towards her wide-eyed figure, pulling his shirt-tails loose and lifting his chin. 'Would you mind?' he murmured as he came to a halt well within the limits of her personal space. 'The collar is so tight and the buttons so small, my big clumsy fingers always have difficulty manoeuvring. Would you undo them for me?'

He waited passively, his big, clumsy fingers innocently hanging at his sides, and after a brief hesitation Anya reached up, going on tip-toes to see what she was doing so that she could comply with his request as quickly and efficiently as possible. He turned out to be right about the buttons. They were devilishly playful little things and she was aware of his warm breath stirring the hair at her temples as she slid her fingers inside his snug collar to help work the fastening loose, her knuckles massaging the hard column of his throat, the unique, spicy scent of him rising from his warm shirt as he lifted his arms, infusing her with familiar longing.

Suddenly she became aware of the reason that he had moved. The strategic pins anchoring her elegant French twist were plucked out and her hair tumbling in a silky, sun-streaked spray down her back.

'What did you do that for?' she demanded, struggling with the second and last tiny button as his arms fell back to his sides.

'You were frowning and I thought that maybe your hair twisted up like that was giving you a headache,' he said innocently. 'You don't wear it up at night, anyway, do you?'

He meant in bed. 'Sometimes,' she lied.

'But not tonight,' he said with a bone-melting satisfaction.

'There!' She tried to step back but he caught her hands.

'You haven't finished…' Holding her eyes, he moved her fingers down to the first button below his collar. 'Please…' he said softly, and, mesmerised by the smouldering desire in the blue gaze, she undid it for him, only to have him slowly guide her hands down to the next button, and the next, and the next…each act of compliance acknowledging his bold intention to seduce.

'Do you recognise it?' he murmured, as they reached the last button and her fingers brushed against the betraying bulge that pushed at the front of his trousers under cover of the loose shirt.

'Recognise what?' she said, blushing furiously, recklessly tempted to trace the outline of that intriguing hardness.

'My shirt…it's the one you borrowed that night to cover your peek-a-boo charms,' he murmured, sending a fresh flush of awareness through her body. 'I've discovered I like having something that you wore next to my skin. It's as if you're wrapped around me, caressing me with your featherlight touch every time I move…'

His shirt was fully unbuttoned now, exposing his powerful chest with its masculine pelt of crisp, dark hair arrowing down over the hard ridges of his abdomen to a thin tracing below his navel. He placed her hands over his hard, flat nipples.

'Would you like to do that to me, Anya?' he invited in a whispering groan. 'Would you like to touch me, stroke me, wrap yourself around me and move with me, on me….' His hips shifted as he spoke, pushing at her skirt, teasing her with their mutual awareness of what she was doing to him.

His skin was hot to the touch, taut and seductively smooth under the roughening of hair, she discovered as he released her hands to roam in helpless fascination over his upper body. It was as if she had never touched a man before, and she hadn't…not with this combination of excitement and fear, hunger and yearning, not with a mingling of love and bittersweet resignation, knowing that there was not even the pretence of love in return and not caring… For the moment it was enough that he wanted her, that right here, right now, she was the most desirable woman in the world to him.

When her fingernails scraped over his nipples he shuddered and let out a thick groan. The harsh sound in the quiet luxury of the lounge startled her and her confidence faltered. Was she mad? What had made her think she could handle an affair with such a formidable man?

'I—what if Petra gets up?' she said, backing away. He shadowed her with a smile that had her skittering nervously towards the two adjoining doors on the opposite side of the suite to Petra's room. 'I think it's time I was in bed—'

'You're right, of course,' he agreed smoothly, looming up behind her and putting out a hand to cover hers as she grasped the first door handle. 'Wrong room,' he purred in her ear, his other hand sliding around her waist, drawing her back against his naked chest.

'I—it's very late,' she tried.

'Yes, it is…far too late for either of us to back out.' He nuzzled the side of her neck through the fine veil of her hair, nibbling at her tender skin and licking at the tender lobe of her ear. 'I've been thinking about this all night…and so have you,' he said, compressing his swollen shaft against the soft curve of her bottom. 'About what we were going to do when we were finally alone together. You've been readying yourself for me, honey…I can feel it, taste it, smell it on you…'

Her head fell back against his shoulder. 'I don't think I'm cut out for this kind of affair—' she gasped as his hand slid up under her lurex top, to dip into her lacy bra and toy with her stiff little nipples.

'How do you know what kind of affair it's going to be until you give it a chance…?' he said, pulling her hand away from the door and drawing it back against the rigid muscles of his hard flank. 'Give *me* a chance to make love to you and you might find that our *affair* is exactly what you need.' He spun her around in his arms and picked her up, carrying her into his room and dropping her down in the middle of the huge bed. He locked the door and swiftly stripped off the rest of his clothes.

Big, hard and naked, he approached the bed where she was still kneeling in a state of delicious confusion. 'Take a good look, honey, it's all yours,' he drawled at her furiously blushing face, and she seemed bewitched by the bold arousal that jutted from the dark thatch of curling hair between his strong thighs.

She moistened her dry lips. 'You're—you're very—'

'Well-endowed?' He grinned wickedly.

That, too! 'I was going to say arrogant,' she said shakily, unable to tear her eyes away from his glorious nudity, beguiled by the supreme naturalness of his attitude to his flagrant sexuality. 'Whatever happened to the slow dance of seduction?'

His smile was a slow sizzle. 'Afraid I'm going to rush you? Not a chance! I still have you to unwrap and I know that's going to be the most fun of all…' He crawled onto the bed, prowling towards her like a sleek, glossy-skinned predator, enjoying the game as she retreated up against the stacked pillows, snatching up the handmade chocolate which had been placed on the turned-down covers and holding it out to him in laughing protest.

'You think that's enough to satisfy my sweet tooth?' He licked his lips and took a bite of the chocolate, following it up with a swift lunge and a bite at her mouth. His hands cupped her face, the velvety-smooth chocolate melting on their mingled tongues as he spilled her backwards across the width of the bed, his leg pushing heavily between hers as he plundered her willing mouth.

All Anya's former doubts and fears vanished like mist under the blazing sun of his hungry passion. The willingness to love was a strength, not a weakness, and it was worth all of the pain she was probably storing up for herself to have this chance to express her love in its most intimate physical form, to be at one with the man to whom she had secretly lost her heart. No, not lost...*given*. Even if Scott didn't know it, tonight he was going to be truly well loved in the fullest sense of the words.

He held her beneath him, protecting her from his full weight by the strength of one arm, his initial urgency reining back to a lazy exploration of the tender crevices and most pleasure-sensitive areas of her face and throat. For a long time there was only the hush of whispered praise and the soft susurration of sighs and kisses, the rustle of clothes against skin.

There was something fiendishly erotic about being pinned, fully dressed, to a bed by a naked male, and soon it was Anya who was frantically trying to hurry the pace, stroking her hands over his chest and back, drawing her nails up through the hair on his thighs and caressing his lean, muscled buttocks. Her mouth released from bondage to his, she squirmed down to taste the musky hot skin of his chest, but it wasn't until her tongue brushed his bronzed nipple and her tentative touch fluttered against his satiny-hot manhood that Scott exploded into passionate action.

He peeled off her tight lurex top, his eyes searing her with his approval as he traced the edge of her scarlet quarter-cup bra with his tongue and kissed and nipped his way over the soft mounds that swelled above the cups, paying special attention to the nipples that peeked at him over the indecently low-cut lace. 'Tell me you were thinking of me when you put this on,' he growled against her creamy flesh, hooking his finger into the underwire between the padded cups and dragging the fabric down so he could suckle at both cherry nipples unhindered.

'I...yes...you...' Anya struggled for coherency as he abraded the moist, glistening tips of her breasts with the light stubble on his jaw before unclipping the frothy concoction and tossing it away, the better to enjoy his delectable feast.

'Oh, God…Scott…'

'Aren't I going slow enough for you?' he taunted, and drew back to flip off her dainty black sandals, his hands sliding up under her skirt, groaning with pleasure as he discovered the silky bare skin at the top of her thighs. 'Stay-ups!' he sighed, running his fingers around the elastic top of her stocking. 'Doncha just love 'em?'

His mingling of passion and humour was as seductive as his sultry provocation and so obviously such a startling new concept to Anya in bed that he delighted in turning their love-making into a joyous romp that left her both breathless and quivering on the edge of completion as he stripped off the tiny, damp thong that barred his entrance to the moist haven of her desire and settled himself heavily between her slender, stockinged thighs.

Then the laughter was swept away in the power and glory of his surging possession and Anya could only cling to the rock-solid shoulders, her fingers slipping in the sweat of his shuddering exertions as he thrust deep into her wet, creamy depths, establishing a driving rhythm that exploded into a mutual rapture of the senses, his mouth drinking in her helpless cries of ecstasy as he claimed her heart, soul and body for his own…

CHAPTER EIGHT

ANYA opened her eyes just as dawn began to filter in around the thick curtains that protected the penthouse suite from the importuning world. She lay on her back, her blonde hair spread out in a wild tangle on the pillow, the ends tickling at the chin of the naked man who lay sprawled on his stomach beside her, his arms cushioning the pillow under his head, his face relaxed in deep, satiated sleep.

If she had been inclined to disbelieve the evidence of her eyes there was the evidence of her body to attest to the mind-blowing fact that Scott Tyler had spent the night in her bed...or, rather, she in his. She ached in the sweetest of ways in the wickedest of places. The crisply laundered white hotel sheets were wildly rumpled, draping low across their bodies, and, looking down, she could see the tiny bruises and abrasions of love on her breasts and stomach.

Carefully easing over onto her side, she studied the sleeping man, blushing to note that he, too, had reddened marks on his shoulders and back, as if he had been attacked by a fierce small animal...as indeed he had! His hard mouth was relaxed and slightly swollen, throwing the small scar into prominence, and that, along with the break in his arrogant nose and the tousled hair and strong growth of his beard, made him look rakishly disreputable and utterly desirable.

She knew that she would never have any regrets about giving herself to him because he had given of himself so generously in return... He had made her feel more like a woman in one night than Alistair had in all the time she had known him. He had been fierce, dominating and passionate, but exquisitely gentle too, and when she had cried after the

149

sheer intensity of that first time he hadn't embarrassed her by asking her why, had just held her trembling body against his and kissed away the tears, and then shown her other ways for them to find pleasure in each other that were less unrestrained but no less satisfying, until she had once again been ready to fling herself into the lightning-storm of emotion that accompanied his tumultuous possession.

It hadn't taken him very long to recognise her lack of experience, and she felt a tingle of excitement prickle over her bare skin as she remembered how much he had enjoyed teaching her the different ways in which her body could accept him, excite him and bring them both to rapturous completion. He had liked to watch the shocked delight appear on her face each time he'd given her a new kind of caress, to coax her into using her hands, her hair, her mouth to make his body quicken and see her shyness melt away in a ravishing eagerness to torture and torment him until he was wildly out of control.

Oh, no, she needn't have worried that he would find her too *ordinary* in bed. He seemed to have no concept of the word. With Scott she had been made to feel supremely special, unique, exquisitely fashioned to satisfy his desires in a way that no other woman ever could, or would...

A smile stole across her lips as she lovingly studied his sleeping face, resisting the temptation to brush the dark strands of hair off his brow and kiss the faintly pouting mouth. So wary and mistrustful when awake, he was determined not to let himself be vulnerable to love. His daughter had cracked the self-protective shell around his heart, but the small breach wasn't wide enough to admit anyone else, had merely thickened the scars created by past betrayals.

Scott had been extremely vocal in the throes of passion, but not a word had been permitted to pass his lips that Anya could mistake for a profession of love. The profound sense of completeness that she had experienced in his arms was a gift that she couldn't acknowledge without jeopardising their relationship. Well, he might not be interested in *her* gift of love, but there were other things that she could give him that would bring him a joy that he *was* prepared to accept.

She began to ease back towards the edge of the bed, sliding out from under the covers, taking care not to awaken the sleeping tiger. Her feet soundless on the thick carpet, she snagged his shirt from the chair as she passed and scampered into her room, where she had a quick shower and donned the items that she had secretly purchased while Petra had been choosing her dress. She cleaned her teeth and ran a brush through her hair and emerged from her bathroom intending to tiptoe back into Scott's room, to find him sitting on the end of her bed dressed in a hotel bathrobe, a resolute expression that was distinctly unlover-like tautening his face.

'For a moment I thought our night together had been a figment of my imagination,' he said roughly. 'Didn't your good manners tell you that it's not the done thing to flee your lover's bed without at least the courtesy of a farewell?'

Oh, God, was he remembering the way that Kate had taken off without a word? Did he see it as a rejection of everything that they had shared? Did he think Anya was ashamed of what they had done and was seeking to pretend it hadn't happened?

Suddenly his sweeping gaze took in her feet and he did a shocked double-take that would have made her giggle if she hadn't been so unnerved by his brooding words. His widening eyes travelled with excruciating slowness up from the white ankle socks to his barely buttoned silk shirt veiling her delicate curves, the shadow of a triangle at the juncture of her thighs and dusky circles at the centre of her breasts making it obvious that she was wearing nothing at all under the tissue-fine fabric.

'I was just coming back to give you your wake-up call,' she said huskily, emboldened by the flare of his nostrils and the nervous jump in his throat as he swallowed, his incredulousness turning into smouldering recognition. 'But I wanted to get dressed first...as you can see.' She extended a leg, wriggling her toes in the white sock, allowing the silk to flirt slyly between her thighs.

She began slowly walking towards him, shaking back her long hair, causing a rolled-up sleeve to slide off one bare shoulder, revealing the paler skin of her breast.

'Oh, God, I think I've died and gone to heaven,' he murmured thickly, but she hadn't finished with him yet.

'I think there's still a price-sticker on my socks,' she said sweetly, coming to a halt between his spread knees. 'Would you mind peeling it off for me?' She lifted her leg and placed her foot daintily in his lap, just below the loosely tied towelling belt, her heel parting the edges of the bathrobe as she leaned forward.

His spine snapped back as the tender arch of her foot settled into his groin, cupping his rapidly growing arousal. He groaned and grabbed her ankle in a vice-like grip, his other hand stroking up over her smooth knee. 'I don't see any sticker,' he growled.

'You're not looking in the right place.'

He was staring at the tantalising shadow where the tail of his shirt draped over her hips. 'I'm looking exactly where you intended me too, you little minx.'

She felt deliciously wicked. 'What an old-fashioned term. I thought you were a ruthlessly modern man,' she teased, curling her toes against his thrusting resistance.

'Hussy!' he said, holding her foot securely in place, tilting his hips to increase the pressure on his engorged fullness as his other hand continued to creep up her thigh. 'If you're deliberately trying to drive me wild, you'd better be prepared to take the consequences.'

She veiled her smug smile of satisfaction with coyly fluttering lashes. 'How was I to know you were kinky for white socks?'

'Because I told you what a turn-on they were,' he purred. 'And obviously not only for me...' His fingertips had stirred through the fluff at the top of her thighs, finding the dewy feminine flower they were seeking, and he watched her eyes glaze over as he delicately stroked apart the moist petals and insinuated himself into her velvety sheath, his thumb playing lightly over the swollen bud bursting forth from its protective hood.

Anya's insides turned to hot syrup. Her teeth sank into her lower lip and her supporting leg began to tremble, her head suddenly too heavy for the slender column of her neck as sensation rioted through her body.

'Not so sassy with me now, are you, darling?' he murmured, deeply gratified by her extravagant response. He withdrew his glistening touch to pull her astride his powerful thighs and smothered her mewed protest with his hungry mouth, his hands wrenching open the buttons of the shirt and helping her to push aside his bathrobe so that he could crush her bare breasts against his hot chest. He fumbled in the pocket of his bathrobe and she had a dizzy moment to appreciate his forethought before he was ready for her, tilting his pelvis as he cupped her hips, teasing her with a few blunt nudges of his rigid shaft before forcing her slowly down onto his engorged length, merging them into one indivisible being.

Anya moaned at the blissful stretching of her body, winding her arms around his strong neck, trying to burrow further into his kiss. He reefed his fingers through her hair to tilt her head, running his hands down her back to settle at the base of her spine. 'It gets even better,' he whispered. 'Lean back for me...' And when she did he feasted at her breasts, tugging wetly on the nipples as he timed his powerful thrusts to perfection, grunting as her fierce convulsions ignited his own orgasm and they peaked in a wild conflagration of the senses that would be burned into Anya's memory for ever.

'Mmm,' he said lazily as they lay panting in exhaustion on the covers, still damply entwined, amongst a tangle of silk and towelling. He licked at a tiny bead of perspiration on the side of her desire-softened breast. 'We've made love in the bed, the shower, the chair and on the floor in my room...so I suppose we should do the same here.'

Anya's stomach quivered. 'We haven't got time. Petra will probably be awake soon.'

He propped his head on his hand. 'The door is locked. And I can be quick as well as slow. You seem to like it either way.' He chuckled as she pinkened.

'I still think we should be careful. Your— Petra's mother wouldn't like it if she was exposed to—'

He cut her off with a kiss on the mouth. 'Petra's a very intelligent and perceptive girl. She likes you and she's already picked up that I'm attracted to you—or, rather, have the "hots" for you, as she so tactfully puts it. As long as we act naturally about it, she's not going to be traumatised if she realises that our relationship has advanced to the level of being openly affectionate.'

His mouth was being more than affectionate! 'You said you were taking the hotel room so I'd be bright-eyed and bushy-tailed for school today. At this rate I'll be falling asleep in class,' she chided him.

'Ah, but I didn't say that it was *sleep* that was going to brighten your eyes or fluff up your tail,' he teased, riffling the cluster of curls below her flat abdomen with his knuckles.

'You're a very conniving man,' she said, pushing away his hand.

His blue eyes crinkled. 'But would you call me selfish, rude...indifferent to a woman's needs?' he asked slyly.

'*Extremely* rude,' Anya told him, her lips trembling into a smile that made her muted grey eyes glow. He knew very well that she couldn't criticise his performance on the other counts.

'But not offensively so,' he said, startling her with a hint of seriousness. 'I didn't hurt you in any way, did I? I wasn't too rough?'

She couldn't account the damage done to her heart. 'Of course not—'

'It's just that you're rather little, and I can see I bruised you,' he brooded, touching a tiny dark shadow on the upper curve of her breast with a gentle finger.

'You didn't exactly come out unscathed yourself,' she said lightly. 'You don't need to feel inhibited because of my size—'

'*Inhibited?*' That sparked a smile. 'I thought it was my *lack* of inhibition which might have been a problem.'

'Well, it wasn't. I may be little but I'm not brittle.'

'No, you're as pliant as a young willow,' he agreed. 'Quite astonishingly flexible.'

'Don't you ever think of anything but sex?'

'Not when I'm lying on a bed next to a beautiful naked woman—'

'I'm not entirely naked,' she pointed out mischievously. 'I still have my tiny little white socks on.'

He groaned. 'Don't remind me.'

'And you don't have to pretend that I'm beautiful, either,' she told him gravely. 'I'm happy with who I am.'

'So am I,' he said, tucking a strand of hair behind her ear. 'Because who you are is a lovely, complex young woman full of grace, candour and wit, and with an inner strength and intrinsic goodness of heart that makes me feel guilty for taking advantage of her...'

Her breath caught in her throat. 'Is that what you're doing?'

'I wanted Petra to see the concert but my primary reason for inviting you along was to give me the opportunity to seduce you,' he said flatly, almost as if he wanted her to recoil in disgust.

Anya widened her eyes in droll surprise. 'No, really? And here I was thinking that you were the kind of man who *always* carried that many condoms around with you!'

He scowled. 'If you were expecting sweet-talk and romance from me, you certainly didn't get it.'

She actually thought he had been extremely honey-tongued, but she knew what his words were intended to convey. He was warning her against seeing him as love's young dream.

'You must be confusing me with someone who cares about those things,' she said steadily. 'Someone who prefers glamorous trappings to the real thing.'

He reacted with defensive speed. 'If you're talking about Kate, you're wrong. I told you, I could never confuse you— you're as different as day and night. I knew that if you heard about the affair that it would taint your whole attitude towards me—'

'Is that the main reason you kept quiet about it? Because it might have made me suspicious of your motives for seducing me?'

His scowl darkened, his blue eyes sullen. 'You might have thought I wanted to revenge myself on her by taking you to bed,' he admitted reluctantly.

Anya's brow wrinkled, as if the idea had never occurred to her. 'I don't see quite how that would work. I'd think that she'd be more likely to pity you for trying to replace her spectacular self with her drab little cousin—'

He jerked up to brace himself over her body on bunched arms. 'Dammit, stop running yourself down like that! I hope you're not one of those people who excuse any behaviour on the grounds of genius. However brilliant and famous Petra becomes I would still expect her to be considerate of other people's feelings. Can't you see you're a thousand times better than that selfish bitch, Kate?'

'Well, *I* can...but I thought you might be a little hazy on the exact figures,' she murmured, secretly stunned by the genuineness of his anger.

He blinked, his temper stopped in its tracks by her gentle ribbing. A brief expression of uncertainty flitted across his face and her glowing smile widened.

'I don't expect real life to meet the standards of a romantic ideal, Scott,' she said, reaching up to touch his firm mouth. 'Besides, romance means vastly different things to different people...especially men and women.'

'What does it mean to you?' he asked curiously, settling back down against her.

'Well, great music and great sex are a pretty terrific beginning...' she said, straight-faced.

He laughed. She loved to make him laugh. All the harsh, straight angles of his face tilted into slants and curves.

'What does it mean to you?' she dared.

'Right now?' He lowered his head and nudged her nose with his to tilt her mouth up for his kiss. 'Why, you, of course...'

Fortunately Petra slept soundly until Scott went in to wake her, and she was too busy enjoying the novelty of a room service breakfast and emptying the snacks out of the minibar to notice Anya's self-conscious air as she buttered her croissant and poured the coffee and tried to carry on a politely innocent conversation with her wickedly uncooperative lover.

She couldn't *help* but notice, however, when the Jaguar slid to a stop at the school gates and, after turning his head to say goodbye to Petra in the back seat, Scott leaned over and gave Anya a leisurely kiss on the mouth in full view of the school crossing patrol.

'Uh-uh—no tongues, you guys. Remember my fragile juvenile psyche!' she snorted, slinging her bag over her shoulder and opening the door.

'Your psyche could be marketed as a bullet-proof vest,' replied Scott drily, sending her off covered in grins while he kindly tilted the rear vision mirror for a flustered Anya to repair her smeared lipstick.

'A pity it doesn't taste as good as it looks,' he remarked. 'I like you better totally *au naturelle*. Except for the cute socks, of course,' he added, just for the pleasure of watching her blush. 'I've got them in my pocket. You can put them on for me again later...'

She sternly repressed the hot thrill his words gave her. 'You shouldn't have kissed me like that,' she told him, putting the lipstick case back in her bag with a little snap.

'How should I have kissed you, then? I hate to disappoint.'

As if he could! 'Didn't you see them all *looking*?'

'Who? The kids? We're a couple. Couples kiss each other goodbye.' *We're a couple.* The phrase sounded much less transitory than *We're lovers*, thought Anya wistfully. Some couples who never got married nonetheless stayed together all their lives.

'Everyone's going to find out about us anyway. Don't expect me to skulk around with you like Ransom did—'

'We never *skulked*.' She roused herself to say with dignity. 'We were discreet.'

'Although you're employed by the Board he's effectively your boss,' he went on, shaking his head. 'Office affairs are a legal minefield. Ripe grounds for sexual harassment suits, disputed promotions, unjustified dismissals and all sorts of other nasty complications...'

She realised he was enjoying himself. 'We were *not* having an affair.'

'But you were heading that way. Why else would he take you out to dinner on Friday night?'

'Perhaps purely for the pleasure of my scintillating conversation. Men and women *can* simply be platonic friends, you know.'

His lawyer's ear detected a subtle inflection in her tone and instantly pursued it. 'Is that what he told you? That he wanted to keep it platonic? When did he say that—before Friday night—or afterwards?'

'During,' she sighed, knowing he wouldn't rest until he had dragged it out of her. As soon as they had been seated in the restaurant Mark had revealed that the purpose of his invitation had been to tactfully define the limits of their relationship. He didn't want to lead her on, he'd said, and his friendship was all that he could ever offer.

'Much as I really like you, Anya, it just puts me in too much of an awkward position, ethically speaking, to get romantically involved with anyone on the staff,' he had explained, with just the right touch of regret. 'I don't want to go through something like this again. And neither, I suspect, do you...'

Since Anya had been going to say much the same thing herself, she'd hardly been able to get up and walk out in a huff as he had rambled on about how much he valued her as a friend. After all, she wouldn't even have agreed to the date with him at all if she hadn't been jealous of the fact that Scott was going out with Heather Morgan.

Of course, she didn't tell Scott that part. He was already looking far too smug.

'So we both got dumped by disillusioned suitors on Friday night.' He grinned. 'Leaving no untidy loose ends to get in each other's way. We are well matched, aren't we?'

So much so that the next three weeks were a revelation to Anya. Scott might deny any pretensions to romance but he was intrinsically aware of how to make a woman feel special, and being the target of his exclusive interest made her increasingly self-confident, her heart soaring with hope in spite of her attempts to keep her feet firmly on the ground. She didn't get hearts and flowers from him, but she did get handmade chocolates and pretty scented candles and flourishing seedlings for her garden—small tokens of his caring that she cherished more than diamonds.

At first Anya tried to hold back, wary of encroaching onto forbidden emotional ground by appearing to require more of his attention than he was able or willing to give, but he would have none of it, his innate curiosity and natural possessiveness coming powerfully into play as he responded with renewed determination to conquer any hint of restraint in her manner.

That first night he had driven over to see her after Petra had gone to bed—having paid Mrs Lee an exorbitant amount to stay on and babysit—and had ended up banishing the fevered memory of her bathtime fantasy by replacing it with even more ravishing reality. Sleek and playful as a seal in her steaming bath tub, Scott had proved her willow-like pliancy and his sexual athleticism to their ultimate satisfaction, and the detriment of her bathroom floor!

That had set the pattern of their relationship. Most nights of the week she either went over to The Pines for dinner with Scott and Petra, or he visited her later in the evening. They didn't always make love, although the passion between them grew rather than diminished with familiarity. Sometimes they would merely talk, and in the process Anya learned more about him to love. She found out that he donated large sums of money to a scholarship fund to enable some of Hunua College's poorer students to go on to further education, and that he provided free legal counselling to a woman's refuge. She discovered that he had spoken to Lorna and Ken to assert his right to provide his daughter with a trust fund for her education and music studies, and that he was dreading the rapidly nearing date of Petra's departure.

'It feels as if I'm losing her all over again, just when I'm starting to really get to know her,' he said, as they drank coffee on the couch in her living room, Anya curled up against his side, after an exhausting weekend showing Petra the sights of Auckland, including a ferry-ride out to Rangitoto Island in the Hauraki Gulf and a steep walk up to the top of the volcanic cone for a look at the view.

She leaned her head comfortably on his shoulder. 'It's not like last time. You're not really losing her. You've both made a binding connection, you'll see each other again.'

'Yes, this time Lorna's not going to have everything her own way,' he said grimly.

The only point of real conflict between them was Anya's adamant refusal to stay the night at The Pines, or even allow Scott to make love to her there. Neither frustrated argument nor seductive persuasion could pressure her into changing her mind. Her heart longed to make itself at home in *his* home, but she was afraid that in doing so she would be overwhelmed by the intensity of her feelings and relinquish the last remaining thread of control that she had over the progress of their affair. She used Scott's need to concentrate on his daughter in the short time they had left together as the reason for her reticence, but they both knew that it was more than that, and that when Petra had gone she would no longer be able to hide behind her altruistic excuses. The moment of truth was fast approaching—not least because she was also piling up increasingly querulous e-mails from London and Paris.

It arrived far sooner than Anya anticipated. One Saturday morning Scott had to respond to a call for an unscheduled court appearance for one of his remand clients and urged her to stay and keep Petra company while he was gone.

'I shouldn't be too long. By the way, do you know anyone called Russell Fuller?'

Anya shook her head. 'Is he a local?'

'He's a freelance journalist. He rang me earlier to ask if he could come and see the house and pick up some information about Kate Carlyle's time here—'

'Oh!' Her heart nearly leaped out of her throat.

He looked at her, eyes narrowing at the sight of her contracted pupils. 'So you *have* heard of him?'

'*About* him…just that some journalist was doing a big cover piece on Kate. She warned me that he'd probably be coming round,' she said dully.

He frowned. 'Well, I certainly don't want to rake over old ashes, but evidently Kate told him I bought The Pines from her. God knows what *else* she saw fit to tell him. He was fairly insistent that I could help him on the phone, so I thought it wiser to agree to see him and find out exactly what he wants rather than encourage his persistence by turning him down cold. I made an appointment for him to come over this afternoon. It's up to you whether you want to be here or not…'

He kissed her warmly before he walked out of the door, misreading her feverish clutch of desperation for one of entrancing eagerness, leaving her standing on the brink of a deep, dark chasm.

She should have told him…but she hadn't. She had been afraid to destroy the precious trust that had been built up between them. And now it was too late. Her period of grace had run out.

Did she owe her first loyalty to Kate—selfish, brilliant Kate whom she had known all of her life but found difficult to like? Or to Scott—a man whose true complexity she was only beginning to appreciate but whom she already loved? Family or lover? Whichever way she chose someone would be hurt. The question was, which choice would wreak the least damage on the least number of people?

The chunky wooden ladder into the attic still creaked at the metal joints as it unfolded from the pull-down trapdoor, and the attic itself was as dirty and cobwebby as Scott had suggested it would be. Anya's hand shook as she climbed into the cramped, dusty, stifling room, holding up the candle that she had stolen from the dining room to illuminate her way. She hadn't wanted to ask Mrs Lee for a torch, but matches had been a fairly innocuous request that hadn't raised any awkward questions. She hadn't even had to tell any fibs to Petra, because it would take an earthquake to distract the girl from her morning piano practice.

She stepped carefully across the timber beams, ducking to avoid the cobwebs and the low cross-beams that prevented her from standing up. The attic itself was big, running the full length of the house, but only a small proportion of it had been used for storage. Anya didn't bother to look under the bulky, shrouded shapes, holding the candle low to look for the small metal trunk that Kate had described.

She found it tucked against a beam and set the candle carefully down on a peeling paint-pot as she opened the lid, coughing at the cloud of dust that puffed into the air. Kate's green hardback journal was on the top, and she took it out and began rifling quickly through the albums, loose photos and papers, extracting anything in Kate's distinctive slanting hand, occasionally lingering over a half-remembered photograph or amusing piece of family history. Suddenly conscious that the time was slipping away from her, she hurriedly closed the trunk and gathered up her armful of contraband.

As she turned to leave she knocked over the candle, snuffing it out, and realised she'd lost her matches somewhere in the dark. Fortunately the chinks in the roof tiles and the square of light from the open trapdoor guided her stumbling steps back to her starting point and she slithered down the ladder on trembling legs, dropping Kate's journal with a crash on the floor. It fell open and several pieces of paper flew out of the pages, and when she gathered them up her eye was caught by the medical letterhead of a consultant gynaecologist.

She had never meant to read any of Kate's personal papers, feeling that she had already sinned enough against her own honour, but she couldn't help seeing what was right in front of her eyes.

Kate had had a pregnancy test done at the Manukau City doctors' office five years ago. The result had been positive. In view of Miss Carlyle's excellent physical and mental health, she'd had no grounds for abortion under current New Zealand law, even though she was only a few weeks into her pregnancy. If she wished to go ahead with a termination it would have to be done overseas.

Kate, who believed that having babies was the real reason that so few women achieved greatness in the world. Kate, who in the five years since her affair with Scott had recovered from her tax problems and brief career hiccup by fulfilling the promise of her youth with an unbroken string of concerts, recordings and festivals with no more than the odd weekend or two out of the public eye.

No *wonder* she had been panicked at the thought of Scott going through her papers!

'What are you doing?'

Scott looked from the attic ladder to Anya's agonised face. 'My case was called off—the judge was ill,' he explained absently, looking puzzled but not yet suspicious. 'Mrs Lee said she thought you were somewhere upstairs. I heard noises on the way up—I thought we had mice in the ceiling. Was that you? What were you doing up there?' He raised his eyebrows curiously at the untidy stack she was holding against her chest. 'What have you got there?'

In the silence that followed, her treacherous fingers went utterly numb, and the damning piece of paper floated down onto the top of Scott's shoe.

He hesitantly bent to pick it up, along with the fallen journal, alerted by her stillness.

When he saw what he had in his hands he went stark white.

He looked at her again, his eyes pure blue devastation, and she knew that she was looking at the death of a dream.

CHAPTER NINE

Scott didn't say a word. He didn't have to. The dead look in his eyes said it all. Anya felt sick. She could have defended herself against his anger, but his pain defeated her. She knew him now, knew the shocked revulsion he must be feeling at this further evidence of betrayal by someone who had claimed to love him.

He turned and walked away from her, the letter still crumpled in his white fist, the diary in his other hand, moving in a stiff-legged gait down the hall to turn into the master bedroom at the head of the stairs.

Anya went after him. She could do no less. He hadn't shut the door but she didn't take that as any form of encouragement; he was simply functioning on automatic, homing in on his private territory to lick his wounds. He was standing on the far side of the bedroom by the open sash window, flicking through the green journal, sending motes of dust rising to dance through the shafts of sunlight.

Anya had forgotten the burden she was still carrying, and hurriedly set the rest of the letters and papers on the table by the door, her trembling hands smoothing down the sides of her pale pink shirt-dress.

'Scott, I'm so sorry—'

'So Kate left a few incriminating pieces of personal property in storage when she took off, and after what she'd done she didn't have the guts to ask for them back,' he said in a grey monotone, as if he was reading the words off the page. 'Instead she got her sly little cousin to con her way under my guard and see if she could whip the goods out from under my nose.'

His head lifted, his eyes blazing at her from behind their film of blue ice, his intelligence rapidly shaking off his shock. 'How frustrating it must have been when you found I was working from home and Sam was using the room you needed to get into. No wonder you refused to sleep here. The last thing you wanted to encourage was an over-zealous lover who might be inclined to hover inconveniently over every move you made. What a sucker I was to fall for that shy will-she-won't-she act of yours! You were waiting until Petra went home to give you the run of the house. And I thought you were being cautious about committing yourself to something you weren't ready for, when really you were just baulking at the idea of prostituting yourself any more than you had to…'

Anya's throat tightened. This was far too reminiscent of another confrontation they had had, only this time she didn't have her cloak of innocence to protect her.

'I never slept with you for any other reason than because *I* wanted to,' she told him hoarsely. 'All right, so Kate *did* ask me to try and get some things that belonged to her without you knowing about it—'

'And this was your first opportunity to do anything about it? Why risk it now, while Petra was still here?' His face hardened as something clicked in his brain. 'Or perhaps you were afraid this was going to be your *last* opportunity… Ah, yes, of course—' he laughed bitterly '—the magazine article; *that's* the reason for the sudden urgency. My God, Kate knew what kind of dynamite *this* would be if it ever fell into the wrong hands.'

He held up the fisted letter and shook it at her. 'She had the bloody termination, didn't she?' he grated. 'That's why she disappeared so suddenly. She fled to some overseas clinic and aborted my child without even telling me she was pregnant, didn't she? *Didn't she?*'

Anya laced her trembling hands over her sick stomach. 'I really don't know…I can only presume so—'

His mouth contorted into a savage twist of contempt. 'You *presume*—you know damned well she did. She accidentally got pregnant and Kate, being Kate, only thought of how it affected *her*. God forbid she be trapped into any connection with me after I'd already passed my use-by date. I was simply a fling to while away the time while she waited for her agent to get her out of the financial jam she was in—'

'I didn't know anything about it until I saw that letter, just now,' said Anya shakily. 'She simply told me there were diaries here that she didn't want you or the journalist to find…'

'And you accepted that without question?' he sneered. 'Do you think that your gullibility excuses you? You didn't see anything wrong with what she asking of you? The thought that it was underhanded, dishonest, didn't bother you—?'

She moistened her pale lips. 'I—of course I knew it was wrong, but she's family. I may not have been entirely open with you, but I never lied to you, Scott—'

'Oh, come on, actions can lie as easily as words. I knew you were holding back on me but I didn't know *why*. Now I do—*this* was in the forefront of your mind the whole time we were together.' He threw the book and crumpled ball of paper contemptuously onto the floor. 'Dammit, if she'd simply *asked* me I would have been happy to be shot of any reminders of her,' he said bitterly. 'Is she really so arrogant that she imagines I care either way about her any more?'

Of course she was.

'She said she was afraid you might use anything you found as payback—'

'Kate, afraid? Face it, Anya, she was using you, and you knew it and still went along with it. She was demonising me out of guilt, but why didn't *you* trust me enough to be honest? Or is that part of the reason you were holding off—hoping to build up the illusion of trust between us until I was sufficiently softened up to *give* you whatever you wanted, instead of you having to find it yourself?'

He reeled around and spread his arms wide against the sides of the sash window, leaning his forehead against the glass.

'My God, what is it about me and the women I—?' He faltered briefly, his voice harshening. 'The women I seem to attract? First Lorna, then Kate…now you. I've had two lovers who stole children from me and a third who conspired to cover up a dirty little secret. And don't try and tell me that it's a woman's right to choose what happens to her own body—maybe it is, but if it's a principle worth fighting for why do it the way Kate did? With no discussion, no question of choice on my part, or joy for the miracle of life we created together—just get rid of my baby as if it was some kind of minor biological inconvenience. At least Lorna had the decency to consult me about her pregnancy and give me the *semblance* of a choice about my child's destiny.'

She felt his searing words like a brand upon her heart.

'Kate could have just had a miscarriage—' Anya offered up the faint hope. She moved across to stand behind him, the rigidity of his body making his navy suit sit as stiffly across his shoulders as an expensive suit of armour. Unable to resist the urge to comfort him, she laid a gentle, compassionate hand on his unyielding back. His iron-hard muscles contracted even further at her touch.

'You don't believe that any more than I do.' He wiped an angry hand across his face before spinning around. 'By God, Anya, if you're pregnant don't even think of trying to get away with not telling me about it,' he said savagely, his eyes shining with a ruthless intent. 'You may not think I'd make a very good parent but you're not going to be the third woman in my life to deprive me of being a father to my own child.'

'I would never do that,' she said thickly, over the tears in her throat.

'How do I know what you're capable of doing? For all the time we've spent together I don't know you at all, do I?' he countered jaggedly.

'You can't believe I'd ever do anything to harm a baby of yours,' she said, her grey eyes soft and pleading, her hand going instinctively to her stomach in an unconscious gesture of protection that sent a tormented spasm across his angry face. 'And I have no doubt at all that you'll make an excellent father one day. I'm sorry that I let Kate mix me up in her problem, but I honestly didn't know how to resolve it.'

He had been struck a blow to the very foundations of his pride. She took a deep breath, knowing that only by baring her own heart to him could she go some way to healing his wounds, and salvaging her self-respect.

'It wasn't lack of trust that stopped me from confiding in you. It was lack of faith in my own feelings. I believed that I owed my first loyalty to my own family but then I fell in love with you and everything got confused—'

'*Love?*' The word was uttered in loathing. 'You and your cousin say that so easily, yet you don't begin to know the meaning of the word...'

He thought this was easy for her?

'The more I loved you the more angry and jealous I felt of Kate, until I was afraid that my judgement was being clouded by malice,' she pushed on unsteadily. 'So I dithered over what to do until it was too late. I can only say I'm sorry for deceiving you. I love you and I was afraid of losing you, so I pretended to myself that nothing was wrong. I hoped that you might come to feel something for me, too.' Her voice cracked a little but she didn't stop. 'I was so afraid of doing or saying anything that might shorten our time together that I was a coward. I'm ashamed of what I did, but nothing can make me regret loving you...'

'Nothing?' The acid bite of the word warned her that worse was to come. He wanted to hurt her, as he had been hurt, and she had just handed him the perfect weapon. She only hoped that she was strong enough to survive the attack without permanent scars. 'Are you sure about that?'

She lifted her chin, slim and defiant in her silky pink dress, her arms straight at her sides, her fingernails digging into her palms. 'I'm not ashamed of how I feel about you.'

'Prove it.' His eyes glittered with cruelty as he threw down the gauntlet. He walked over to the door and kicked it shut, turning to lean against it with folded arms.

She licked her dry lips. 'What do you mean?'

'You know what I mean. Give me a demonstration of these so-called loving feelings. Let's see how unashamed you are. Take off your clothes. I want you to make love to me as if you really mean it. Show me how much you *love* me.'

She swallowed, refusing to be shocked by his sardonic crudeness, knowing that was what he wanted. 'I won't let you cheapen what we had—'

He shrugged, shouldering away from the door. 'I knew you wouldn't do it. Love has its limits as a form of manipulation, doesn't it, Anya? People have a nasty habit of expecting you to back up your words with actions.'

He stopped in his tracks as Anya's trembling hands went to the top button of her dress. He watched her as she undid the first button and then the next two, revealing the lacy white camisole she wore underneath. They were both breathing hard by the time she got to the button at her waist and he suddenly caught her wrists in both of his with a savage curse, preventing her from going any further.

'Are you really prepared to humiliate yourself like this? For what? It won't change anything,' he railed at her, dark blood flaring on his cheekbones.

'I thought you wanted me to prove my feelings for you,' she said, a tremulous hope stirring at the knowledge that he had stopped her from abasing herself. She bent her head and kissed one of the hands that was gripping hers. 'How can loving a man I respect and admire be humiliating for me?'

He wrenched his hand away and plunged his fingers into her pale, silky hair, pulling up her head to snarl in wounded fury, 'All you're going to be proving is that we don't need to trust each other to have good sex.'

He dragged her against his chest and crushed her mouth under his in a lustful, passionless kiss. Anya remained passive as he ran his hands over her open dress, fondling her braless breasts through the satin camisole and stroking her thighs with a clinical expertise and calculated lack of feeling that made her long to weep.

Instead, her heart aching, she lifted her hands to tenderly cup his angry jaw. At her delicately tentative touch he groaned a harsh protest, and suddenly the quality of the kiss was changing, from aggressive and punishing to a sensual, hungry meshing of mouths, his bullish stance shifting to support her softening body, his hands moving more slowly, a different kind of heat and tension beginning to build up in his big frame. Anya shuddered and uttered a soft cry as he stripped off her dress and began feasting on her soft flesh, shrugging out of his jacket and shirt and tearing at the fastening of his trousers.

'This doesn't change anything,' he groaned again as he pulled off her clinging panties and pushed her down onto the bed.

'I know…I know it doesn't,' she reassured him huskily, welcoming him with parted thighs as he came heavily down on top of her, offering him the only kind of love he was willing to accept. Passion flared and, conscious of the banked anger that had intensified his naturally dominating sexuality, Anya yielded ardently to his every command, their coupling hard and fast, yet deeply satisfying.

Afterwards, instead of lying with her in his arms in the

sweet aftermath of their love-making, he got up before the sweat had cooled on his body and silently tossed Anya her clothing. They both dressed swiftly, Scott substituting casual trousers and a clean shirt for his suit, Anya stealing glances at his unrevealing face, and when they were ready to leave she was stunned when he detained her at the door.

'Are you forgetting something?'

He turned to get Kate's untidy stack of belongings and handed them to her, including the journal and crumpled piece of letterhead.

'Isn't that what you came here for?' he said coldly, as she looked at him uncertainly. 'Take them. They're of no interest to me. They're a dead issue. Just like your cousin.'

And me? She didn't dare ask. At least he was being civil...barely. Surely that was a good sign?

'What are you going to tell the reporter?' she couldn't help asking as they walked down the stairs.

His knuckles whitened briefly on the banister rail. 'As little as possible.' They reached the foyer and he shot a cuff and looked at his watch. 'He's due at two. Tell Petra I'll be out until then.'

'Where're you going?' asked Anya involuntarily. She had hoped they might talk.

He looked at her and she saw a glimpse of tightly smoth- ered rage. He had expended some of his anger in bed, but the rest was festering inside. 'I'm not answerable to any woman, least of all you,' he crunched. 'Don't think your *feelings* give you any sway over mine.'

'I wasn't suggesting—'

'Good. Don't.' He yanked open the front door.

'Would you still like me to stay with Petra?' she scraped up the courage to ask, taking heart from the fact he was still talking to her.

'You're a glutton for punishment, aren't you?' he rounded on her roughly. 'What do you want me to say? What I would *like* is for you to get the hell out of my face! Right now I don't want you anywhere near me, my home *or* my daughter. Is that explicit enough for you?'

The slam of the door reverberated through the big house.

'Jeez, did you and Dad have a fight?' Anya turned to see Petra frowning at her from the door of the music room.

Anya simply nodded, massaging at her temple

Petra padded up the hall. 'A bad one?'

'Pretty bad.' Anya was afraid she was going to burst into tears. 'Your father said to tell you he'd be back around two. I'm afraid I have to leave—would you mind telling Mrs Lee for me?'

She rushed to find her handbag, juggling the papers against her chest as she hunted out her car keys.

Petra followed her out to her car. 'But you will be coming back some time, right?'

Anya's fingers tightened around the keys. 'I'm not sure…'

'You're still going to be doing my tutoring, though?'

'I'm not sure about that, either. I don't know if your father will want me to do that any more.'

'You mean the fight was *that* bad?' Petra was shocked. 'You guys aren't going to break up, are you? But Anya— you can't. I'm going home next week. What about Dad? You know he's going to be all bent out of shape about it. And if you're not here he'll be left all alone…'

Anya was having difficulty seeing through the growing blur. Why wouldn't the key go in the lock? She took a wild stab and to her relief it finally fitted. 'Your father's a grown man. He lived here quite happily by himself before you came along, and he has plenty of friends.'

'Yeah, but he's sorta got used to having people hanging around—you know, like a family.' She caught the car door as Anya got into the driver's seat. 'And what about the puppy we chose?'

Anya looked at her foggily. 'Scott is giving you a *puppy*?'

What a ridiculous gift to buy a child who was about to fly back to Australia. Or was it supposed to be a lure to bring her back for future visits?

'Not me...you! Dad said you told him that you were thinking of getting a dog so he and I went out and bought one for you. But we couldn't give him to you yet because he has to stay with his mother until he gets big enough to be on his own and Dad wants it to be a surprise for you. He's real cute and cuddly, but he has a pedigree and everything, and Dad's even got you a collar and doghouse and a bowl and stuff. He'll still give it to you, won't he?' Petra worried.

A puppy? Scott had gone out and chosen a warm, cuddly squirming puppy for her?

That was the warm, squirming thought that kept popping into Anya's mind throughout a sleepless night and the long, dreary, lonely, grey Sunday which followed.

Giving someone a puppy wasn't like handing them a box of chocolates, she told herself. An animal required a serious commitment from the gift's recipient and that implied serious intent on the part of the gift-giver. That Scott had cared enough to want to buy her a pet to love and laugh and romp with in the grass surely meant that he had more complex feelings for her than he had been willing to admit. Otherwise, why bother? She had made it quite clear she had been happy with chocolates and candles. And doggy people were warm and loving. You didn't give a dog to someone unless you felt they were trustworthy enough to look after it properly.

At that point in her tortuous thinking she always came to a painful cropper. You could have trust without love, but it was impossible to love someone that you couldn't trust. And she was afraid that she had now indelibly associated herself in Scott's mind with the other two women in his life who had badly abused his trust. Sure, once he had thought it over he would probably understand why she had acted the way she had, and hopefully even forgive her, but it was bound to have a negative impact on their relationship. If she had told him that she loved him *before* he had found out what she was doing, things might have been different, but why should he believe someone who had already perjured herself by her actions and omissions?

No, whatever slim hope she had had of persuading Scott that she was worthy of his love was probably gone. But, as he had cruelly demonstrated, a lack of trust didn't stop him having sex with her. If she indicated she would accept such a one-dimensional relationship he might be willing to oblige. The idea left a bitter taste in her mouth. For her, sex and love had always been two sides of the same coin. She hadn't required Scott to return her love before she shared her body with him, but she *had* needed his respect to balance the emotional scales. Now she was afraid she didn't even have that.

Several times her hand hovered over the telephone, but if she rang him, what could she say? *I was thinking about you?* He must already know that. *I want to talk to you?* He would know that, too. As difficult as it might be, she had to wait for him to make the next move. And there would be one, because he wouldn't be able to leave the loose ends dangling. If nothing else he would have questions he wanted to ask, for in the heat of anger he was the one who had done most of the talking. He might have told her to leave, but he had stopped short of telling her never to darken his door again. He also knew all that he had to do was crook his finger and she would come eagerly running.

There was Petra, too; she was bound to be strongly partisan on Anya's behalf…

Her violently see-sawing emotions left her feeling tense and miserable, and by early Monday morning she was so firmly in the grip of a depression that she did something that she had never done in her life—she threw a 'sickie'. So it seemed like fate when, not long after leaving a message on Liz Crawford's answer-machine to explain that she was unable to come into school, she had a phone call from Russell Fuller and found herself talked into being interviewed later in the morning. She would have liked to fob him off with her supposed illness, but she decided gloomily that she might as well get it over with.

Talking to him reminded her she hadn't responded to any of Kate's nagging e-mails, so before he arrived she sent off a terse message to say 'mission accomplished' and ask if Kate wanted her to courier the package or send it by registered mail. Anya would have been quite content to throw the whole lot in the fire.

Russell Fuller turned out not to be the sleazy, ferret-faced scandal-monger she had feared, but a stocky, russet-haired man who not only recorded their conversation on microcassette but also took meticulous notes in his own form of shorthand in a lined notepad. He showed her the faded photo albums he said had been found for him at The Pines by Scott Tyler, after Russell had convinced him that Kate had said they were probably still in the attic of her childhood home.

Anya breathed a sigh of relief as he had immediately moved onto his list of questions, most of which were directed at identifying old photographs, and eliciting anecdotes of Kate's childhood on the farm and in New York. Anya kept her answers brief and to the point when the journalist moved on to her cousin's adult life and personality, but it was his final, casual, off-the-cuff question as he switched off his tape recorder that totally threw her.

'So…this is a kind of circle of fate thing with you and Scott Tyler—him being the owner of Kate's old home?'

'I beg your pardon?' she said warily, wondering if this was some cunning journalist's trap.

'Well, you and Tyler are in love, aren't you? I thought it would be a natural progression.'

'Who told you that?' she asked sharply.

He tucked his tape recorder in his briefcase. 'Tyler did, on

Saturday. He was very co-operative about letting me look around The Pines. Told me Kate had been a sharp negotiator over the price of the house, but he seemed more interested in talking about you than her.'

'He told you I was in love with him?' she asked numbly. A total stranger, and a reporter at that? The bastard! He must have still been rawly furious when he got back from wherever he'd driven.

'Ummm, no, not exactly—actually I think it was the other way around,' he staggered her by saying, leafing pedantically back through his notebook to the reference.

Anya nearly fell off her chair.

'What—*exactly*—did he say?' she asked tensely.

'You want the full quote?' He consulted his notebook. 'Here it is...ummm...' He pondered his squiggles, making a few seconds seem like several centuries. 'Ah, yes: "Kate was certainly a stunning woman, but it's her cousin I fell in love with. Anya has a kind of quiet grace and inner beauty that hits me square in the heart every time I see her. I think some part of me recognised that on the day we met, and I loved her even before I knew I was capable of it." Not a bad turn of phrase. The guy could be a writer himself.'

'But he said that to you off the record, right?' she said in a strangled voice.

'Nope. Got it on tape, too.' He tipped her a sly grin. 'Why? Would you like me to make a copy of it for you to replay to him every time you have an argument?'

He had been clearly looking forward to the offer of a second cup of tea, but instead found himself unceremoniously bundled out of the door.

Anya's finger was shaking as she punched in the numbers on her kitchen telephone from the business card in her wallet. 'I'd like to make an appointment to see Scott Tyler, please. Today. My name is Anya Adams.'

The businesslike voice on the other end was professionally

regretful. 'I'm afraid Mr Tyler is working reduced hours at the moment and he doesn't have any free appointment slots for the rest of the day. He's booked right through until he leaves at four o'clock.'

Anya clutched the phone with both hands. 'But he *is* in the office?'

'Oh, yes—but as I explained, Miss Adams, he doesn't have any spare—'

'Thank you.' Anya quickly put the receiver back in the cradle, cutting off a hasty cry.

'Oh, wait—Miss Adams—'

Remembering the adage about dressing for success, Anya took the time to select her clothes carefully and took extra care with her make-up and hair. She got into her car looking what she hoped was serene and confident, but tension and excitement took its toll and her cool became slightly unravelled in the hour it took to drive to the huge Manukau City shopping centre where Scott's chambers were located. It was another anxious fifteen minutes before she found the tower block she was looking for and somewhere to park, and in the express lift her stomach seemed to arrive at her destination well before she did.

The professional offices of Tyler & Partners weren't as intimidating as she had expected—the reception and waiting area actually showing the impact of natural good taste rather than cutting-edge interior decoration. The atmosphere, too, was informal and, by the look of the comings and goings and the number of people flicking through glossy magazines in the waiting room, business was good.

Squaring the jacket of her classically cut powder-blue suit, she approached the reception desk, eyeing the politely enquiring face, calculating whether haughty assumption or confiding friendliness was going to work better.

But when she opened her mouth, the young receptionist spoke first.

'It's Miss Adams, isn't it?'

'I—yes.' Was it someone she should know? A former pupil, perhaps?

'Julie!' The receptionist waved another, older woman over. 'This is Miss Adams.' She mouthed the next two words rather obviously. 'For Scott.'

'Oh, yes, of course.' Anya recognised the voice she had spoken to on the phone. 'Thanks, Melissa. Miss Adams? This way, please.'

Anya found herself whisked along to the end of the corridor, unprepared for the ease and rapidity of her progress.

'But, I—don't—'

'—have an appointment. I know.' The woman gave her an amused look. 'Scott came in just as I was telling you he was all booked up. I must say he described you to a "T".'

Anya frowned. 'You mean he's expecting me?'

'Well, if he wasn't he will be now. Melissa just buzzed him to get rid of his client.'

Anya clutched her cream handbag. 'I don't want to put anyone out. I thought you might just manage to squeeze me in when he had a few spare minutes...'

It was too late for cold feet. She was already being ushered into a large office to see Scott closing an adjoining door, spinning around on the plush green carpet to face her.

He looked wonderful, she thought fretfully. While she had been suffering from a thousand cuts of guilt he had been burnishing his skin and glossing his hair and generally making himself look like a million dollars. And there was no sign of joyous welcome in his eyes, just a watchful reserve.

'Crime obviously pays,' she said drily, looking around the office.

'The defending of it certainly does. It's a growth industry. Did you come here to assess my net worth?' he drawled.

She bit her lip and gripped her bag harder, reminding herself that she had it on very good authority that she hit him in the heart. Unless he had been making an ironic joke.

'No. I'm sorry; I don't know why I said that.'

'You're nervous. Sit down.' He indicated the chair in front of the desk, but instead of going around to the leather swivel chair when she had seated herself, he sat on the edge of his desk, legs relaxed, extended and casually crossed at the ankles, arms folded across his chest. He didn't look as if he had a nerve in his big, gorgeous body, damn him!

'Why aren't you in school?'

'I called in sick.'

He dropped his hands to the desk, gripping the edge on either side of his hips. 'You're ill?' he asked, searching her delicate face.

Sick with love. She looked away from his penetrating gaze and shook her head. 'I just felt like a day off.'

'And you've come to spend it in my office? Or have you come for my professional advice? If you're going to take up housebreaking as a full-time job you'd better put me on a retainer. You don't seem to have much talent for the job.'

Her heart quickened at the wry amusement in his voice. If he could joke about it...

'Russell Fuller came to see me a couple of hours ago.'

'Did he, indeed?' A lazy eyebrow rose, but she noticed with another skip of her pulse that his fingers were tightening under the overhang of the desk. He wasn't any less nervous than she; he was simply better at disguising it.

'Yes, he did. And he told me certain things. Things that you said to him. About me and you,' she said defiantly. 'Were they true?'

'What do you think?'

She looked at him in silence, torn by hope and fear. Suddenly she was tired of being brave and feisty, and her eyes began to sting.

'I think if you have to go through a third party to tell me

what you feel, that doesn't bode very well for our future relationship,' she whispered, a tear spilling down her cheek.

He instantly lunged forward. 'Oh, God, no—don't cry—' He grabbed her out of the chair, and drew her into his strength, rubbing up and down her back with his big hands. 'Please—don't cry— Of course they're true, Anya. I was wilfully blind not to see it before. Of course I love you. That's why all this hit me so hard. When I was talking to Fuller it just suddenly all fell into focus, and then I spent the rest of the weekend agonising over it, figuring out why I'd been so anxious to lash out, to push you away, and blame you for things that weren't your fault. You said you were afraid of losing me—imagine how terrified *I* felt. This is all new territory for me. I've never, in my whole adult life, had anyone to *belong* to, or belong *with*—I've always felt like a loner. And then Petra came along, and you burst into my life—you, who'd been hovering around the edges of my mind for months, making me feel itchy and angry and *aware*. I built you up in my mind as someone I couldn't want, but then I wanted you anyway. My heart was already setting me up for the fall. Even when I seduced you I knew that you weren't the kind of woman to sleep with a man without feeling some deep emotional tie, but I couldn't help myself.'

His arms tightened possessively around her, as if trying to absorb her into his very being. 'And you turned out to be the best thing that ever happened to me. The one who made me feel that I *wanted* to belong—I wanted to be a husband, a father, and I wanted to be those things with *you*. Deep down I knew you were nothing like Lorna or Kate—it was just a form of panic, the shock realisation that you could hurt me far more than they ever had—it was the old protective reflexes kicking in. But I can't live in that kind of vacuum any more. I need you to love me, and I promise I'll learn to be more open about the way I feel—you can teach me. So please, stop crying now. I didn't mean to make you cry,' he said, pressing desperate kisses all over her damp face.

'Well, what did you expect me to do?' she sobbed into his chest.

'I don't know—yell at me, slug me one, laugh...' He groaned. 'I thought you might find my way of telling you I loved you quirky—romantic—'

Her head jerked back. *'What!'*

He smeared a tear away from her cheek with his thumb. 'You know—like sending a troubadour, to serenade you...' he said ruefully.

'Are you *crazy*?' she demanded.

'Yes, of course I am—crazy over you. Why else would I do such a stupidly juvenile thing? Fuller told me on Saturday he was intending to try and see you on Monday so I rang him last night at his hotel and *asked* him to tell you what I said.'

'Why didn't you just come over and tell me yourself?' Anya was trying hard to be angry him, but it was difficult with so much joy in her heart.

He bowed his head against her shoulder. 'I was ashamed,' he confessed, his voice muffled in the curve of her neck. 'You'd told me you loved me and I'd thrown it back in your face. I called you a prostitute, and then treated you like one. I used sex to try and show you that you meant nothing to me. I thought you might hate me for that and I was afraid to face you. I thought: How can she possibly love a man who treats her that way?'

She sniffed, shaken yet reassured by the depth of his anguished self-doubt. 'It's a dirty job but somebody's got to do it.'

He lifted his head to receive her glowing smile of benediction. 'And that someone has to be you,' he vowed. 'Only you.'

'Hmmm.' She spread her hands across his chest and

looked up at him, her nose pink, her rain-washed grey eyes loving. 'What are the pay and conditions?'

'No pay, but plenty of rewards. As for the conditions: you have to marry me, come and live at The Pines, let me seduce you out of your scandalous underwear every night, have my babies, be a stepmother to my brilliant, smart-mouthed daughter and fill my house with all the love and laughter it can hold.'

'And a puppy?' she bargained slyly, plucking at a button on his waistcoat. 'A family isn't complete without a family pet.'

He hesitated, a secret smile in his voice as he conceded, 'Maybe a puppy. But only if you're good.'

She tilted up her face to him, her hands sliding down under his jacket to settle down around his hips as she insinuated the centre of her body against his, pushing him back against the edge of the desk. 'Oh, I'm very, *very* good...' she purred.

His eyes smouldered and his mouth came down on hers, and as she allowed herself to be swept up in his loving passion she blissfully contemplated just how very badly she was about to misbehave....